SPECIAL MESSAGE TO READERS

This book is published under the auspices of

THE ULVERSCROFT FOUNDATION

(registered charity No. 264873 UK)

Established in 1972 to provide funds for research, diagnosis and treatment of eye diseases. Examples of contributions made are: —

A new Children's Assessment Unit at Moorfield's Hospital, London.

•

Twin operating theatres at the Western Ophthalmic Hospital, London.

•

A Chair of Ophthalmology at the University of Leicester.

•

The establishment of a Royal Australian College of Ophthalmologists "Fellowship".

You can help further the work of the Foundation by making a donation or leaving a legacy. Every contribution, no matter how small, is received with gratitude. Please write for details to:

THE ULVERSCROFT FOUNDATION,
The Green, Bradgate Road, Anstey,
Leicester LE7 7FU, England.
Telephone: (0116) 236 4325

In Australia write to:
THE ULVERSCROFT FOUNDATION,
c/o The Royal Australian College of Ophthalmologists,
27, Commonwealth Street, Sydney,
N.S.W. 2010.

THIS SAVAGE LAND

Devastated by the murder of his wife and son, Joe Bradley rode blindly into the wilderness, seeking oblivion — or even death. However, when he discovered that death at the hands of the Shoshone Indians involved torture and mutilation, he realized that dying wasn't easy. He found the choice facing him was either to become a fighting man or a dead dog. Strangely, the actions he took brought him in the end to justice.

Books by Johnny Mack Bride
in the Linford Western Library:

THE MEN AND THE BOYS

JOHNNY MACK BRIDE

THIS SAVAGE LAND

Complete and Unabridged

LINFORD
Leicester

First published in Great Britain in 1992 by
Robert Hale Limited
London

First Linford Edition
published November 1994
by arrangement with
Robert Hale Limited
London

British Library CIP Data

Bride, Johnny Mack
This savage land.—Large print ed.—
Linford western library
I. Title II. Series
823.914 [F]

ISBN 0-7089-7596-8

Published by
F. A. Thorpe (Publishing) Ltd.
Anstey, Leicestershire

Set by Words & Graphics Ltd.
Anstey, Leicestershire
Printed and bound in Great Britain by
T. J. Press (Padstow) Ltd., Padstow, Cornwall

This book is printed on acid-free paper

1

IT was the water that caused him to stop. That, and a desperate though barely-acknowledged thirst. If it hadn't been for the demands of his physical body he'd have gone on riding till the horse collapsed under him. As it was, his mount was beat, like the pack animal dragging behind him: their heads hung low and their feet trailed grooves in the dust as they dragged themselves along, like animals that had been ignored, neglected and ridden unthinkingly for several hundred miles. As indeed they had.

He slumped in the saddle and stared dully at the landscape before him as the horses trudged on. The ground was rising gradually as he approached the foothills of the Rockies. Quarterway up the next slope there was a little wood, thick here, thin there. The narrow stream glinted on the edge of it. Trees offered shelter, there would be wood for a fire but he did not think of these things: the ideas just went unbidden through his mind, giving him no pleasure, no comfort. He did not even decide to camp but just dully sagged, rolling, in the saddle until his mount dragged to a halt by the water.

For a few seconds more he slouched in the saddle, eyes dull, seeing and hearing nothing, while the animals bagged themselves with water, then he hauled his feet from the oxbows and dropped heavily to the ground. Automatically, from long habit, he loosened the cinches, dragged off the saddle and let it fall to the ground. He moved sluggishly to the pack horse and did the same there. Then he dropped to his belly and drank, like an animal, from the stream. The body's craving satisfied, he heaved himself back from the creek bank and sprawled out on the ground.

The sun was going down behind the trees, the light of the summer night fading. Any other man would have checked his security, seen to his horses, lit a fire, made coffee, stretched his blanket: he did none of these things. He lay almost unmoving, looking into space. After a while he fell asleep. He twitched and turned often and, as the evening air grew cooler, instinctively pulled his shirt round him. The sprawl of his body and the harsh breathing suggested that his wasn't the sleep of rest and repose but the unconsciousness of exhaustion. His horses, ignored and relieved, tore wearily at the welcome grass.

He lay in the stupor of fatigue for two or three hours, while the sun disappeared and the light gradually faded. Darkness grew all around him. Still he slept but now, with the edges of his exhaustion blunted, something began to disturb his oblivion. He twisted, turned, jerked convulsively from time to time. Low, tortured, moaning sounds escaped from between his clenched teeth. One of the horses bounded in alarm at the sound.

He was back in the nightmare again.

★ ★ ★

He was trapped in a bog, held softly but absolutely from neck to ankles in warm ooze and the men were riding down from the slope to his home. They did not have faces, identities, because he had never seen them. He could not tell how many of them there were, whether they were short or tall but he knew, right down in his guts — the knowledge was eating at his guts like a cancer — that they were purely evil.

His body jerked in violent spasms as he tried to break free from the cloying, warm-wet hold of the dream-bog. Pitiful, begging moans forced themselves from between the clenched teeth, causing the uneasy horses to stop grazing and lay back their ears, showing the whites of their eyes.

He could not understand how the bog figured in his dream. In fact he had been at Fort Dodge, on farm business, when the men had come, had been sitting in the cantina there drinking with friends when the men had arrived at his homestead near St Aubrey, Kansas. But here, in the dream, he was in a bog, held relentlessly in a warm, comfortable ooze as the men drifted down on his home like buzzards on a helpless, new-born fawn, to pick the gentle eyes out and tear the soft, new flesh.

They were in his yard now, dismounting, looking around them in pleased appreciation at the trim corral, the good horses, the tidy log cabin.

He struggled dementedly, knowing it was futile, to break out of the stranglehold. In the dream Mary had come to the open door, was studying the men uneasily. She had her red check dress on and an apron over that. She was mixing stuff in a bowl — the cake for little Joe's birthday. Two of the men had guns in their hands. They were looking for him, or for any man that happened to be around: they wanted to make sure they were safe and to satisfy their desire to kill. But he was not there: he was trapped and could only watch it all happen.

Mary opened her mouth to speak but some of the men simply rushed her, shouting joyously. They carried her off her feet, the mixing bowl falling to the ground, the stuff for the birthday cake spilling out. Now they had her on the ground and were covering her with their bodies as she struggled and screamed and frantically called his name. They were laughing and swearing loudly, tearing her clothes off. One was sitting on her head now and holding her arms, another straddling her, exploring her body with savage joy. A loud wail came from the cabin as the five-year-old boy inside sensed the violence; the horses milled uneasily in the corral, frightened by the sound.

Two men were still searching for any man who might be around. They had guns in their hands and wanted to use them. But he, who should have been there to protect his family, was safely absent.

The sleeping man jerked in violent desperation. One man was raping Mary now, fiercely but leisurely, grinning at his laughing companions, panting out his pleasure. Mary's animal howls drew the guts out of the man in the dream as he struggled hopelessly to escape.

The nightmare was reaching its hellish climax. Joe, aged five, had rushed to the door to see what was happening. With a wail of angry terror he rushed at the men assaulting his mother, clawing at them with all his puny strength. The man sitting on Mary's head shoved him laughingly aside. The boy flung himself back into the attack. The man shoved him away again with his left hand and, swearing with annoyance, drew a pistol with his right. As the child flew at him yet again he blasted his life out with a point-blank shot.

Now the first rapist had risen to be replaced by the second. He hobbled to the house, pulling up his pants, grinning in relief. He went inside, started examining the contents of the cabin . . . stuck his finger in the sugar bowl and licked it . . . picked up one of the cookies that Mary had just baked, bit into it and nodded appreciatively.

He poked around on the shelf above the fireplace, found the cheap painted tin with the few dollars in it that Mary saved on the housekeeping money. He nodded brightly and stuck the money in his shirt pocket. He began casually sacking the house, strewing the bedding over the floor as he searched for hidden money, making a careful choice of items of clothing, a coat here, a Stetson hat there, a pair of boots.

The second man was raping Mary now, another sitting on her head, holding her arms. Her body jerked uncontrollably and she hoarsely screamed her husband's name. The man sitting on her head eased himself off, drew his pistol again and dealt her a murderous blow to the face. She went limp, unaware of the rutting man violating her.

The first rapist was in the corral now, choosing a horse. Another man had gone into the house and was ransacking the place. A third man was feverishly pulling off his pants.

The sleeping man struggled incessantly as the nightmare went into its last act. The men were leaving now. One man was throwing kerosene over the furniture in the cabin — and here the body jerking on the creek bank heaved in thrashing hopelessness and the sounds that forced themselves out between the clenched teeth were like the death howls of a wolf. Another man was lighting a torch of paper and sacking. They all had fresh horses . . . His horses.

They were shouting to each other. The last man came out of the house.

Mary stirred on the ground, an untidy pile of bloody rags. Some of the men were mounted, others still tightening cinches. The mounted men wheeled their frightened horses. One man threw the torch into the house. There was a trail of sparks. The men began to ride off raggedly, yelling hysterically. Fire began to flicker, slowly . . . it crackled, grew redder . . . smoke billowed out of the door. There was a loud, soft, explosive 'Huff' and the cabin burst into a mass of flames.

* * *

There was more stirring amongst the pile of bloody rags on the ground. A figure clawed its way up to a crouching position . . . Mary . . . three-quarters naked. She scrabbled around like a wounded animal . . . saw the burning cabin, flames blossoming ten feet high . . . rose with an insane wail and staggered unsteadily, one shoe off and one on, towards the house. She stopped suddenly, realizing that the cabin was not a house any more but a funeral pyre. She staggered around drunkenly, saw the bloody body of the murdered child and the last of the raiders settling himself in the saddle and flew at him, screaming, in a furious act of demented anger, clawing at him with hands like talons. He drew a pistol and clubbed her round the head, again, and again, literally beating her to the ground. Still she held on to his stirrup, so that she was dragged a dozen yards from the house. Then he spurred his horse savagely, causing it to bound and break her hold. He galloped off screaming a savage war-cry and she slumped lifeless to the ground.

There was an un-human cry from the figure lying by the creek-bank and an almighty jerk and he broke free into wakefulness. He trembled, crouching on the damp earth, looking frantically about him but not recognising his surroundings. So he remained for several minutes.

After a while he realized that he had been in the nightmare again, as he had last night, and the night before, and the night before that, ever since it had actually happened and he had ridden away from Saint Aubrey, away from Kansas, away from it all. Or tried to ride away from it all.

He sat shivering in the cold night air, trying to let his mind become blank. But the human body has its own needs and its own ways of satisfying them, independently of the human mind: his body reacted automatically to the cold: unconsciously, his hand reached out and took hold of the blanket lying by his saddle and dragged it across his shoulders. So he sat, for nearly two hours, seeing, hearing nothing, sunk in a dull stupor.

Would the nightmare never give up its hold on him? How long ago was it now? How far had he ridden from that feared and hated place? He didn't know, didn't care . . . but he had been riding a long, long time. He'd had to get away from the place, couldn't stand being near his former home.

Neighbours had tried to be kind, but who could have stayed there, with that knowledge, with those memories? People had talked of the law, the sheriff, justice, but nobody had seen the men, nobody could have identified them; it was unlikely that they'd ever be caught.

When he had first learned what had happened he had tried to kill himself, tried to shoot himself with the Springfield, but somehow he just couldn't do it. Something away deep down inside himself wouldn't allow him to pull the trigger. When he'd tried — and he'd tried many times — it was as if his arms and hands had become paralysed. So he had stayed sorely alive, tortured continuously in every part of him that was capable of feeling.

He shivered violently and huddled closer into the blanket. How could he live with ninety per cent of his life gone? His wife, half of his life? His son, all of his life! How could he bear the desolation, the terrible irreplaceable loss, the permanent emptiness, the uselessness of living?

Yet he hadn't been able to end it all, and after several attempts he had simply got on his horse and ridden away from there, not knowing or caring where he was going, simply riding off into the wild, unsettled country of The West.

It was dangerous country too. Not like the country around Saint Aubrey, Kansas, which enjoyed the protection of Fort Dodge. It was the year 1844 and America from the Missouri west to the Pacific was an immense virgin wilderness, as wild and fierce and unsettled as the darkest heart of Africa. Here forts were few, and very far between; hostile Indians hunted the territory; wild beasts abounded — bears, cougars, wolves — and there were the other wild beasts, the even deadlier kind, the renegade whites who prowled the trails, away from any form of law and order, living by the gun and the knife, living on the lives of others.

Any other man would have been very careful in this situation, would have been constantly on guard against being killed: this man didn't care; he was indifferent to any threat of death; in fact, if he had looked deep down into himself he would have found an actual desire for death, a hope that someone might do for him what he had been unable to do for himself.

So he sat now, in his wretchedness, on a creek bank in what would one day be western Colorado, and wondered what would become of him.

Gradually fatigue overcame him. He slumped backwards on to the damp earth and fell asleep again. It was poor quality rest; his body twitched and jerked and pitiful, frightening moans forced themselves out from between his grinding teeth.

When the light grew again he woke

up, sat up and remained for nearly half an hour, sitting where he had fallen the previous evening, staring into space. Then he rose stiffly, drank from the creek and went to catch his horses.

One, his saddle horse, was close by. He led it to where his saddle lay and hefted his rig aboard. His hand reached into the saddlebag and found a piece of jerky. He shoved it unthinkingly into his mouth and chewed mechanically as he fastened the cinches. He went back for his pack-horse, loaded it dully, mounted and kicked his horse into motion.

The animals plodded on, finding their own way, following the bank of the creek. Up a long, steep rise they went, the horses labouring and breathing hard. Near the top they paused to breathe and he let them.

The route they had taken had brought him to a point above and behind the place where he had slept the previous night. His eye rested on it dully for a minute then he dug his mount in the ribs with his heels and pulled its head round.

It was then he saw it: two piles of horse dung, lots of it, in two neat piles, as though two horses had stood side by side for a long time, several hours. It was fresh too, green, and very, very recent. Without knowing why, he dismounted stiffly and examined the ground. Trampled considerably by hoofs . . . cropped very short where the horses' heads had been. He studied the ground around that area. There were bones there . . . just a few . . . small bones . . . rabbit, maybe? No. They were too big for rabbit bones. Dog? An unpleasant shiver ran through him. Indians ate dog, didn't they? He studied the bones closely. They were almost bare of meat but the slivers that did remain suggested that it had been cooked. The owners of the horses had been eating, though there was no sign of a fire. People had been here, and had stayed here for a considerable time, their eyes towards the place where he had camped . . . towards him, perhaps.

As usual, thoughts went unbidden through his mind. Why had they been watching him? Who were they? Indians? Why hadn't they attacked? Maybe because of the noises he made during the night? He knew he made noises, could hear them, was frightened by them, although he was powerless to stop them.

So he was in Indian territory. No surprise. Must have been in it for days. Wonder he hadn't seen signs of them before. His knowledge of geography was scant but he knew he was in the foothills of the Rockies. Hadn't he once heard an old prospector say that the Sioux and the Arapahoe held this land? And weren't there Shoshone, or something like that . . . and Crow? He didn't know about Indians, wasn't a fighting man. He'd been a farmer, a sod-buster . . . most he'd shot was rabbits . . . but he was sure he'd heard of these tribes . . . and what he'd heard hadn't been good.

He remounted and rode on, his mind only slightly more active. It didn't mean they had been watching him. They might have had other business. In any case it didn't bother him: if they had come for him a week ago he'd have been downright glad. Even now he was indifferent to danger and the possible threat of death.

Yeah . . . but death was one thing: the method of dying was another. He'd heard about Indian deaths . . . about men found with their eyes gouged out . . . tongues cut out — He tried to stop the thought coming but it forced its way into his mind: 'With their dicks and balls cut off and stuffed into their mouths!'

A cold fear oozed from his spine and flowed across his shoulders and down his back. He felt suddenly that he was very much alone, far from any help or comfort, in a fierce, savage land. It was the first hairline crack of emotion in a shell of indifference that had protected him for months and, as his jaded horses trudged onwards, this man, who had felt that he had no fear of death, glanced frequently and apprehensively behind him as he rode and he sat much more tensely in the saddle.

2

HE stopped half a dozen times that morning. He told himself that the purpose of the halts was to rest his horses, but he hadn't been in the habit of resting them before, and as he squatted by the side of the trail his eyes continually scanned the route he had travelled.

Once or twice he saw birds fly up suddenly. Did that mean anything? If they had been disturbed by men then maybe there were men half a mile behind him. But he couldn't be sure: he wasn't a woodsman, didn't know the patterns of bird-behaviour. He was a farmer, and the time he'd spent in the open had been spent pushing a plough, labouring hard, striving to build a farm for his wife and family. The thought of wife and family was too painful and he pushed it out of his mind.

So . . . those birds that flew up? Did they mean anything? He didn't know, and because he didn't know he just kept on going forward. He couldn't think of anything else to do.

He stopped again at noon and, squatting by a little stream mechanically chewing jerky, he tried to decide how he felt and what he ought to do.

It was possible that there were men after him — Indians, maybe — who might try to kill him. What should he do?

Was he afraid of death? He examined himself carefully and found that he could honestly answer 'No.' In fact he recognised the truth within himself: he would actually rather be dead than alive. Well, that was all right, then. All he had to do was let them catch up with him. They would do the rest and he would be out of this misery.

Strangely, the conclusion didn't reassure him. It was true that he didn't fear death . . . but he did fear dying. And especially he feared torture and mutilation. He cursed and spat in a mixture of fear, doubt and frustration. Was there no way out of his dilemma?

Well, he couldn't sit here all day trying to work things out; they'd catch up to him, and then . . .

He mounted again and held his horses still for a moment in ragged uncertainty then gently turned them off the rough buffalo trail he had been following and headed into wild, open country and back the way he had come. 'I'll ride back a-ways,' said the voice inside his head. 'Take a look. See what happens.' He hadn't taken a positive decision: his actions resulted from the fact he was *unable* to take a decision. He was doing what men do in such a situation: he was stalling.

He kept well back from the rough trail, riding slowly, uncertainly, and taking advantage of every scrap of cover he could find and he hadn't ridden more than quarter of a mile when he detected movement on the trail. Luckily he was in a thin wood of pine trees, a hundred and fifty yards back from the trail. He dismounted swiftly without thinking, and held a hand over each of his horses' muzzles, not wanting his presence betrayed by a whinny of horse recognition.

As he waited, heart beating surprisingly fast, they came into view and his doubts were resolved.

Indians. Four or five of them. Riding silently on lean, pinto ponies. Almost naked except for breech clouts and wearing feathers in their hair.

He found his breathing becoming difficult. He had seen Indians before . . . even back in Kansas you could see Indians. But the Indians he had seen had been peaceable. Indians . . . horse traders . . . farmers, even. They wore white man's clothes, or something like it and even spoke a little English. But he wasn't in Kansas now, and again the realization flooded over him that he had ventured into a vast, fierce wilderness that was a wholly different world from the one he had inhabited all his life.

These were wild Indians. Savages. As different from the tame Kansas Indians as a starving wolf is from a Boston lady's lap-dog. Their naked bronze bodies glinted in the sun, their faces were painted masks of grotesque cruelty and they bristled with weapons — bows, lances and stone-age axes. Most frightening of all, they pursued their quarry with a fierce, savage intensity which radiated outwards from them and chilled the blood of the man watching. These men were deliberately following something up the trail ahead of them and they intended to kill it.

The only thing he knew that was up there was himself.

He stayed motionless while they passed, partly because he wanted to avoid detection, partly because he was scared into immobility. Even after they had disappeared from sight he remained unmoving, not knowing what to do.

After several minutes the natural urgency in the situation forced him into action. They might come back. If it was him they were after — and he knew it was — they might follow his tracks: he'd heard that Indians were good trackers. For a very brief second he wished heartily that he had never ridden into this wilderness, where there was no-one to help him, but that passed and a calmer, more fatalistic, attitude filled him. He'd better do what he could.

He mounted and rode deeper into the wood, spurring his horse forward urgently, dragging the pack horse blunderingly after him and looking all round him for a suitable place to defend himself. The trouble was that there was no such place: one part of the wood looked just like another — trees thinly spaced, occasional clumps of undergrowth, scattered rocks. He began to grow anxious. They'd be catching up to him soon!

Eventually he settled for a small

clearing containing a jumble of rocks. Two big rocks leaning together formed a deep cleft, almost a small cave, that he could shelter in. At least nobody would be able to come at him from the rear. Thick brushwood surrounded the clearing and he didn't like that . . . it would provide cover for enemies . . . but there was no better place. Besides, there was a little stream nearby: he might have need of water, if he was there some time. He flung himself from his horse, quickly unsaddled both animals and tethered them close to the little rock-cave: they'd be easy meat there, he knew . . . could be killed easily, standing there. But from what he'd heard Indians valued horses and would not willingly kill an animal that they could use. In any case he didn't have time for any choice: they'd be on top of him in a little while.

He dragged the pack saddle and all its burdens over to the rock-cave then dumped his riding saddle beside it.

He drew the Springfield from under the securing ropes on the pack-saddle, checked the load and scrabbled for his priming flask. As he primed the long rifle he wished fervently that someone would invent a gun that could be loaded quickly: you were safe if you had a gun — but once you had fired it you were almost defenceless until you had two minutes to re-load. He was glad he had a pistol too. He brought it out, checked the load and the flint and lock then primed that weapon too. What he would do when he had fired both weapons he didn't know didn't want to think. He got out his axe and laid it down on the ground beside the saddles and the guns. He wished he'd brought a knife . . . that fine big hunting knife that Mary had bought him on their first anniversary, with his name engraved on it. That would have been very welcome . . . but that had gone . . . in the burning cabin . . . with everything else.

He suddenly thought of food and

water and ran to the little stream and filled his canteen full to the brim. He rummaged among his packs and brought out more jerky. He'd been living on only jerky and water for weeks. Funny how, right now, it didn't seem enough.

He backed awkwardly into the little cleft between the two big rocks, sat down heavily and dragged the two saddles in front of him. He laid the Springfield on the pack-saddle, pointing forward, and made sure the pistol was close to his hand. The axe next, lying by his left hand.

Was he crazy? Maybe the Indians weren't after him at all? Well, he would soon know. He took up a piece of jerky and began chewing but his stomach rebelled against the juices sent down to it. Nausea stirred in him erratically and an unwelcome chill invaded his bowels. He knew what it was: it was naked fear.

Suddenly he wanted to piss. He debated the wisdom of getting out of his hidey-hole again and couldn't make up his mind. He sat for five minutes, unable to decide, then rose and clambered out . . . didn't want to be sitting — maybe dying — in a piss-soaked corner of the earth! He stood five yards away, pissing endlessly, hearing imaginary sounds from all quarters and — he recognized it reluctantly — trembling. He scurried back into his corner, his pants uncomfortably wet with the dribbles. Maybe, while he was at it, he should have . . . But no! He hadn't time for that. Jesus! What a situation he had got himself into!

Back in his miserable shelter he laid the Springfield down across the pack-saddle, pointing outwards. He checked the pistol again and laid it down by his right hand. Axe on the ground beside him . . . Now they could come: he was as ready as he would ever be . . . nothing to do now but wait.

He waited. Nothing happened. He waited a long, long time — two hours or more — and nothing happened. He heard every sound that occurred in the world — the rip of the grass as his horses tore at it, the rustling of small live creatures in the brush, the shuffling of wings that birds made in the trees, and, once — a heart-stopping sound — the patter of a larger creature's feet — a deer probably — as it scampered away on scenting his presence.

He remained keyed up to maximum alertness, expecting any second to be called on to fight for his life, but time passed and nothing happened. Slowly, inevitably, his nervous temperature came down. Maybe those Indians weren't after him, he thought . . . or maybe they hadn't been able to track him? Maybe they were peaceable Indians after all? He was in an overwrought state, he knew that — had been for weeks. Maybe his imagination was running away with him?

He began to breathe more easily, although he was careful to keep alert. At least they were giving him a little time. He ought to use that time wisely . . . prepare himself as well as he could. His mind went to the bundles strapped and roped to his pack-saddle. They were the very same bundles that he had brought back from Fort Dodge on that fateful day when his whole world had been destroyed. He had stayed with Eli Jones, his nearest neighbour, for the first week or so after finding his home destroyed, and had never unpacked the load. Later, when he had ridden away, he had automatically taken the pack-horse and its load with him. Maybe there was something in it that he could use right now?

Cautiously, he moved the Springfield off the pack-saddle and groped among the bundles, glancing nervously around him as he did so. It was no use. He'd have to undo the ropes and straps. He moved the long gun to the side and began to undo the pack, which meant taking his eyes off his front. Still, nothing had happened . . .

There was a deep, narrow tin of

gunpowder, about five pounds, he figured . . . he was glad of that . . . and a small sack of lead ball, for the Springfield and the pistol. He felt some relief: at least he had some ammunition. He rummaged amongst the various packages . . . Corn meal . . . coffee . . . horse shoe nails . . . a coil of tough twine . . . a side of bacon . . . salt . . . a sack of flour . . . a bridle, with little brass bells on it, that he'd bought for little Joe . . . for the pony that he'd been going to get for him . . . His heart contracted painfully as the memories came back to him afresh and he would have broken down if he hadn't suddenly remembered that his life was in immediate danger. He laid the bridle aside and reached into the pack again and stopped. Those little bells? Could he make use of them? Did he have time for such elaborate precautions? He pondered, undecided, and went back to his examination of the pack. A new tin pan . . . some flints for rifle and pistol . . . a little flask of gun-oil . . . some new rope . . . two enamel mugs . . . two soup spoons . . . a piece of leather for boot repairs . . .

He stopped suddenly. Those little bells . . . and the coil of twine . . . What if he . . . ? Did he have time? Maybe those Indians would come in the night?

Very cautiously he eased himself out of his tiny shelter. Nothing happened. No arrows hissed through the air at him. He listened, but there were no sounds.

Taking the pistol with him, he took the coil of twine to the nearby brush and tying one end to a knee-high branch, strung the twine, from bush to bush, in a rough circle around the clearing. It took him a long time, and he constantly darted anxious glances around him as he worked and several times he started and whirled round, the pistol raised against an imaginary enemy.

He crawled back into his shelter and

began to pick the little bells off the decorated bridle. It was slow work and, having no knife, he had to make do with only his fingers and the sharp edge of the mizzen of his pistol lock. But he got the job done, and still there were no threatening sounds.

He crawled out again and, going to the circle of twine, tied the half dozen little bells to it at intervals of ten yards. He plucked the twine experimentally and was rewarded by a distinct tinkle from the bells.

He crawled back into his shelter feeling just a shade more reassured. Was there anything else he could do? He thought about the gunpowder. Powder was scarce. Could he afford to use some of it? Grudgingly he laid the tin of powder beside him, close to hand. He'd need light . . . fire . . .

The idea of fire made him think of food. That was funny: he hadn't thought of food for weeks . . . had just chewed jerky, without thinking. He suddenly realized that he'd grown skinny, that his arms were like two sticks. His belly ached for a bowl of stew or cornmeal mush. There was cornmeal right there . . . in that sack.

He crawled out again and nervously gathered some firewood . . . clean, dry stuff, and light . . . luckily it was plentiful. He gathered a good pile. Then he ventured as far as the stream and half-filled the new tin pan with water.

Back in his hidey-hole he realized that he wasn't quite so scared as he had been earlier. Maybe there wasn't really any danger? Still, he'd be on guard. He lit the smallest of fires, a tiny, clear blaze that would give off hardly any smoke, spooned cornmeal into the water and sat in his rock-shelter, with his mouth watering, while he held the pan over the flame.

He ate the thick gruel half-cooked, marvelling that anything could taste so good, then went back to the creek for more water and repeated the process. The afternoon was fading, his belly was pleasantly full and there was no apparent danger. Hadn't he been working openly around the area with no consequences? He'd probably been over-reacting; most likely he was in no danger. He relaxed a little more, and a little more still. His breathing deepened. In a few minutes he was asleep.

He came to immediate wakefulness with a terrifying start and grabbed frantically for a gun, any gun. It was dark. The little fire he had lit was just the merest glow of dull red ash. He stared wildly around him, looking for Indians.

Nothing. He listened, straining his ears. Nothing.

What had wakened him? He was crazy, letting himself fall asleep . . . didn't deserve to live. Something must have awakened him. What was it?

The night around him was innocent. A little breeze sighed in the trees, the gurgling of the little stream could be heard clearly, his horses steadily cropped the short grass. There were no sinister sounds. Goddammit! He was tired! How long could he keep up this constant alertness?

He kept it up all night, or most of the night. In spite of himself he fell asleep from time to time and woke up in sudden anguished fear, scrabbling dementedly for his guns. But the night passed and nothing happened. Then, in the dirty grey-gloom of dawn, a bright tinkling brought him to a terrifying clarity of consciousness and he saw several dark shapes bounding towards him — almost on top of him.

He grabbed the Springfield and fired it while still bringing it up. There was an ear-splitting explosion, a long tongue of orange flame and the nearest figure dropped from sight. He clawed for the pistol, seeing and smelling the furious dark figure that was clawing at the saddles in front of him, stabbing viciously at him with a long lance. His hand found the tin of gunpowder. In pure panic he wrenched the lid off and flung some directly on to the dying fire.

A fierce white light blazed the night and he saw, in one blinding exposure, the painted face, a terrible face, the nose broken, the right eye torn and down-drooping. He grabbed the pistol and fired and saw the figure topple sideways. Suddenly he was out of his shelter with his axe in his hands not knowing how it happened but swinging the axe hysterically around him and crying senseless sounds towards his attackers. Something bit into his arm but he ignored it in his madness. A dark figure was attacking him, whirling at him with a stone-age axe, missing him by inches, forcing him backwards, threatening to overwhelm him. Another dark figure had struggled to its feet again and was staggering away from the fight.

Without conscious thought he ducked suddenly, bending nearly double. He heard the stone-age axe sing over his head and as his assailant hesitated for a fraction of a second he swung his own axe with all his strength at the naked legs in front of him. He heard bone snap and an animal scream tore the air and the figure was sinking before his eyes. He sprang up, swung the axe and battered the figure to the ground, whirled round looking for the other figure he had seen retreating and found himself standing alone, gibbering senseless sounds and streaming with sweat. A loud crashing in the brush told him that someone or something was running away, fleeing for its life.

So he stood for several long minutes, waiting for what didn't come. Around him he could hear groans, thick, snoring breathing. It came from the figures strewn around him on the ground. There was another sound too — a frightened, whimpering sound. It was himself. He was crying.

3

IT must have taken him half an hour or more to come to his senses, during which time he could have been killed several times over. Luckily for him there were no further attacks and eventually his nervous whimpering ceased, his breathing became normal and he sank down exhausted on to the cold earth. He dragged himself back into his shelter, laboriously reloaded both rifle and pistol, and sat there, waiting for his mind to re-form again and tell him what to do next.

It was a slow process. First he became aware of his own hurt. He had been slashed across the upper left arm. A great flap of flesh hung down like a bloodhound's ear, the blood congealing blackly. In wonder, he bound it up as well as he could with a strip of blanket. Then he began to notice that there were two bodies lying out there in front of him, two nearly-naked, brown bodies. Indians. Slowly he became conscious that he had killed them. *He* had! A man who had only ever shot at rabbits before!

He couldn't leave them lying there . . . had to get them out of sight, although the idea of touching them revolted him. He crawled out, pistol in hand, and went to the first dead man. He was sprawled in an unnatural position, his face half-buried in the earth, the mouth gaping, the eyes wide open. There was a big bloody mess of a bullet exit wound in the middle of his back. The other body was crumpled up twenty feet away, one of the arms grotesquely twisted, the head at an unnatural angle, the neck clearly broken.

Again he surveyed the space around him, pistol raised, looking for enemies, but there was nothing there. 'They might come again,' he thought, and then, 'But I've got to move these bodies . . . And if they do come, well, I'll have to fight again, that's all.'

He grabbed the first body by the ankle and hauled. As the body rolled over he saw a knife in the hide belt at the waist. He dropped the cold leg and gingerly withdrew the knife from its buffalo-hide sheath. It was an ordinary kitchen knife, or had been at one time, the sort of knife that women and kids ate their dinner with. It had been honed and sharpened to such an extent that the blade was badly worn and erratically shaped, but it was clearly an ordinary domestic knife. How in hell had an Indian got hold of that out here? But white people *did* come out here, he believed, though they were few. Maybe the knife had changed hands a dozen times in its life and ended up being traded to an Indian. Or stolen. Having no iron or steel of their own, Indians would value such things mightily.

Shuddering with distaste he removed the buffalo-hide sheath from the belt then made a cursory search of the other body. A stone axe lay underneath it, the head secured to the wooden shaft by rawhide lashings, tied on while green probably, and shrunk tight. A long lance lay a few yards away, the war-blade fashioned from an old door-hinge, sharpened to a razor edge and similarly secured to its shaft with rawhide. He collected all the weapons and put them in his shelter.

Moving the corpses took a lot of effort. He had to drag them one-handed through the brush, the pistol ever ready in his other hand, and had to stop frequently through exhaustion. He dragged them as far away as he dared and, having no digging tools, had to leave them lying in the open. 'Wolves and coyotes and buzzards will get rid of them in a couple of weeks,' he consoled himself.

On his way back from the second trip he heard a noise, distinct and loud. He dropped into a fearful crouch, the pistol raised and the noise came again . . . a rustling, trampling . . . and a pinto pony shoved awkwardly through the brush, diligently cropping the short grass. Another followed close by. They both wore primitive bridles of woven horse-hair. Dead men's horses. He caught the bridle of the first and studied the animal. Unshod. Young and fit. On its white shoulder and haunch patches there was a crude imprint of a hand in red ochre. The other pony was adorned with stripes of yellow and blue on neck and rump. He led them back to the clearing and tethered them with his own animals.

He went to the stream and drank. He wondered if he should eat while he had the chance but he couldn't face food. What should he do now? He couldn't go forward: they might be waiting for him up ahead. He couldn't go back: that was as dangerous as going forward. So he was stuck here, for a while, anyway. Maybe he should fortify the place as well as he could in case of further attacks?

Seemed like a sensible thing to do, and he was in need of sense right now.

Rocks might help. There were lots of rocks of all sizes around the clearing. He began by rolling the biggest ones up to his primitive shelter and piling them round it. He built it into a kind of rough cave, bigger and deeper than it had been before. The smaller rocks he piled up in flanking walls around his shelter until he had exhausted the supply of nearby stones, then, pistol always in hand, he began to venture further from the clearing in search of more material.

So he laboured until dusk, stopping only to drink now and then. When he noticed the light fading he crawled into his shelter and drew the saddles in front of him again. He lit a tiny fire but could not be bothered cooking food. He stuffed handfuls of uncooked cornmeal into his mouth and chewed, then after a drink from his canteen stretched out to sleep, all his available weapons ready to hand.

He started awake a dozen times during the night, scrabbling for weapons, but no attack came. The night remained still and silent except for the yelps of coyotes and the occasional hoot of an owl and he soon went back to sleep. Significantly, although he twisted and turned now and then and sometimes ground his teeth, his sleep was less disturbed than it had been for weeks. A new disturbance often drives out an older one, even if only temporarily, and physical exhaustion often drives out everything.

In the morning he woke hungry and resigned. He couldn't go forward or back so he'd have to stay here, at least for the present. He cooked breakfast — cornmeal mush followed by bacon and beans then coffee, using the same tin pan for all the cooking. As he ate he figured. There were lots of young trees around; he could cut them down; it would reduce the cover of any approaching enemy, and it would provide him with the means of building a better shelter. He envisaged a kind of three-sided shelter built of log walls, with maybe some kind of a roof, in case the weather got bad. True, those Indians might attack again while he was at it but he had to take that chance . . . couldn't just sit here and do nothing.

He began right after breakfast, taking all his horses and weapons with him. He stacked the weapons close by and hobbled the horses, letting them graze while he chopped. When he had cut and trimmed a load he harnessed his pack horse to it and, mounting his saddle horse, led the load back to his shelter. By the end of that day he had one wall built. He saw no sign of Indians all day and there was an added bonus: the need to stay constantly alert and the concentration on the job in hand drove the misery of his bereavement temporarily out of his mind. That evening, when he crawled into his strengthened shelter, he felt a little less destitute and miserable than he had for weeks.

He continued his work during the next few days, cutting down young trees, trimming them and hauling them back to his shelter. Gradually a clumsy construction took shape, a three-sided shelter surrounding his rock-cave. When it was completed he decided that it would be better if he put the rocks outside the shelter so he began on that labour. During this period there were no attacks though once he did see some Indians. They were some way off, maybe half a dozen of them. They sat their ponies motionless, as though watching him. They were too far away for him to make out much detail but it seemed as if one of them might be wounded as he appeared to have one arm strapped against his body and he leaned to the side awkwardly when they finally turned and rode off.

So several days passed without incident. The work was taking hold of him, doing him good. He ate well and slept reasonably well, except for some false alarms in the night. It was true that there were times when he would remember his loss, his murdered wife and son, the loss of his farm, of his former life, and he would be stricken with grief, remorse and, strangely, guilt at having temporarily forgotten them.

Some days were better — and some days worse — than others. A good day was the day he decided to put a roof on the cabin. He saw the rough domestic structure rising in the wilderness, the fruit of his labour, and he felt good. A bad day was the day when, half-way through the roofing, he was reminded of the cabin he had built for himself and Mary. The poignancy of the memory was so keen that he broke down and wept openly. All appetite for work left him and his situation once again appeared hopeless and his work futile.

He gave up working in despair and went, shoulders slumped and head hanging, to get his horses.

He mounted, took his other horses in tow and began the dreary ride back to what now seemed to him a lonely hovel. Half-way there, crossing a small clearing, his heart breaking, his whole existence empty of any comfort, he heard suddenly the fierce swishing of grass, the clatter of unshod hoofs and saw that they were almost upon him — about ten of them — hideously painted and bristling with weapons — screaming like madmen.

All thought ceased in him as action took over. He threw up the Springfield and fired point-blank at the nearest of them. The ball went through the brave and into the man behind him and both fell among the fierce, trampling hoofs.

He did a terrible thing then. Letting his led horses go he wheeled his mount, drove his spurs in and galloped straight at them screaming out his own war-cry. His whole being was filled with rage — rage at the way fate and life had treated him, rage at the loss of his wife and son, rage at his loneliness and vulnerability, and mad fury at these beings who were repeatedly trying to kill him.

He saw death appearing in front of him and did not give a damn. 'Let it come!' he thought, and then, 'But since I am to die, let me take some of these bastards with me!'

No man has less to lose than the man who is dead already. He rode at them absolutely without fear, with no regard for his life or safety but filled with a fierce, murderous hate, wanting only to hurt, to kill, to destroy — himself and his tormentors with him.

Somehow he had a stone axe in one hand and the sharpened kitchen knife in the other. He made no attempt to steer his horse but just charged into the middle of the attacking force, stabbing here, battering there, again and again and again, spurring his frantic animal forward always into the thick of the fight.

For minutes insanity reigned — horses

milling madly — the dull sounds of stabbing and clubbing — curses, screaming gibberish — the hoarse grunting of wheeling ponies — the frantic scrabbling of hoofs. One brave toppled backwards from his leaping pony, one hand held to the stab wound in his back; another fell sideways to the ground, his head bloodily battered, two found themselves left behind the fierce battle and, frightened by the ferocity of it, declined to rejoin.

Somehow he had lost his knife and couldn't find his pistol — the world around him was a whirling kaleidoscope of coppery bodies, painted faces and pinto ponies — he was battering everything dementedly with the stone axe regardless of blows to himself — he had a fleeting glimpse of one brave, holding back from the others, not taking part in the struggle but watching, one arm and hand bound to his side as if wounded. For a fraction of a second he recognised the scarred face, the broken nose and downward-dragging eye — then he had the pistol and he fired it into the face of a brave a foot away from him, dropped the weapon, shoved out madly with his empty hand, heaved a brave off his pony and rode over him, trampling him under the iron-shod hoofs, and again he was whirling the stone axe, looking for other skulls to crush.

Suddenly they were fleeing from him. There were no braves around him except those on the ground. The others were galloping away from him, fleeing madly. He saw them escaping and could not bear that it should be so. He spurred madly after them, screaming and cursing. As he pursued them he was fleetingly conscious of one brave who cast hate-filled glances behind him as he fled. The expression on the scarred, misshapen face suggested that he was half-inclined to wheel about and fight it out but he seemed to think better of it and continued his flight, one arm bound to his side and riding perilously, leaning to one side. His dun pony bore the imprint of a red hand on its shoulder.

There was no lessening of their pursuer's fury. The Indian ponies were faster than his exhausted horse but he spurred savagely and caught up with a panicky straggler. He rode right into the back of the fleeing pony, there was a surging, struggling mêlée and both riders fell to the ground. He threw himself on the screaming Indian, a howling, weeping fury ceaselessly whirling a bloody axe, and bludgeoned the life out of him.

He struggled to his feet, still filled with furious destructive rage, but found no fight around him. He wandered around a few bewildered steps, swinging his axe, cursing and panting. One or two wounded Indians were struggling over the ground, writhing in the death-throes or trying to crawl to escape. He rushed amongst them, his steps now heavy with near exhaustion, and clubbed every one to death with the stone-age axe.

It took a long, long time for his sanity to return. When it did he found himself lying on the bloody earth among the dead, and the light fading. His horses, as usual, were grazing unconcernedly nearby, accompanied by two or three new ponies; it was strange how unaffected they were by violence and how quickly they resumed normality.

He tried wearily to rise and felt an agony in his limbs. Struggling to a sitting position he took stock of himself and a new wave of fear flooded over him. There was a great gash seven inches long in his right thigh; it gaped like a great red mouth and blood pulsed freely from it; he could see white tendons and a glimpse of bone deep down inside his leg; he found that he could not see out of one eye; when he tried to move his right arm it would not work; when he turned his head a savage pain racked him: he put his hand up and found a ragged groove torn there, running from his throat, behind his chin and ear and right up into his scalp; blood soaked his clothes; when he opened his shirt he found another bloody graze across his ribs.

What he did next he did in a fear-filled daze. He found the Springfield, untied the cord by which he sometimes slung it across his shoulders and bound it tightly round his gaping leg wound. Somehow he got his shirt off and wrapped it, warm and blood-soaked over the wound. His other hurts would have to wait. Using the Springfield as a crude crutch he hobbled over the battlefield till he found his pistol. He found the knife too, between the ribs of a dead Indian.

He fainted twice before he could haul himself across his horse but somehow, after a long time and exquisite agony, he found himself in the saddle and his pack horse in tow. It seemed to take him hours to ride back to his shelter; several times he had to rein in because he simply could not stand the pain, but eventually he became aware that he was there, that the horse had stopped in the familiar place and that he was still in the saddle. He half-fell to the ground and lay there unmoving for many minutes. Then, ignoring his animals, disregarding his weapons, not caring even about his wounds, he crawled into his primitive shelter, stretched out, and waited for death.

4

THE three riders reined in their weary mounts and paused on the ridge, looking down on the straggle of shacks below and ahead of them.

"That the place?" asked the big man. He sat heavily in the saddle, as if tired. His face was black with dirt, bristle and sunburn, the lower half split with a hare-lip. A big, powerful man, casually sure of himself, he wore thick clothing although it was summer: the travel-stained riding pants hugged his thick legs, a soiled woollen shirt stretched across the barrel chest, a thick coat, heavy with dirt, wrapped him round the great shoulders like a bearskin. He glanced at the man on his right, one eyebrow raised quizzically.

"Well, if it ain't the place, it's one jus' like it."

The man who answered was small, lean and tough, his appearance cleaner, mainly because his colouring was fair and the several days growth of beard did not show so much. Anyone seeing him for the first time might have mistaken him for an ordinary little man, except for the fact that he radiated danger: there was an aura about him of something sinister, unhealthy, something best left alone.

"How does a place like that get to *be* here?" The big man shifted his weight in his saddle and chewed his lip thoughtfully. "I mean, who in hell comes out here to settle down? And how come they stay here, huh? I mean, 'way out here. Miles from . . . well, ever'thin'."

"Maybe that's why they like it," grunted the little man. "Maybe they don't like folks . . . or folks don' like them . . . jus' like us." He gave a wicked little grin. "I mean plenty folks don' like us."

"Yeah . . . " The big man hesitated,

not to be deterred in his healthy curiosity. "But I mean, how do they *live* . . . How do they get all that stuff together . . . them shacks . . . water barrels . . . stove . . . ammunition . . . an' all that stuff?"

"They bring some of it with them when they come out. Like I mean maybe they was goin' to Cal'forny or someplace . . . an' only got this far. So they set themselves up, build a shack . . . "

"Yeah, but how do they *live*?" The big man was positively curious. "I mean, how do they get, say, powder an' shot, after the stuff they brung with them is all gone?"

"I guess one of 'em rides back east a-ways for it," suggested the little man. "Oh, not all the way to fuggin' Missouri!" he added hurriedly. "Jus' to one of the forts . . . or maybe they trade with some of the wagon trains that's startin' to come through. I know they trades with the wagons for some things . . . horses, mules, whisky, feedstuffs, all like that."

"An' with the Indians too," the third man put in. "They trades with Indians." He was younger than the other two, tall, with ragged blond hair and a pale, pasty complexion. His long legs stuck out in front of him, his broken boot soles flapping.

"Yeah, Kowalski?" The big man grinned at him indulgently. "An' what the fug do they git from goddam Indians? Fuggin' scalps?" He laughed loudly, looking at the little man, inviting him to join him.

"Naw, not fuggin' scalps," Kowalski explained matter-of-factly. "They gits . . . well, furs, maybe an' buffalo robes, an' stuff like that. Folks pays money for furs . . . back east, I mean. Yeah, furs is worth money back east."

The big man nodded, licking his hare-lip. "An' you reckon you know the fella that's got this place, eh, Bandy?"

The little man shrugged. "Knew the fella that useta own it. Tobe Bleek. Him an' his son. Been here for coupla years. Course he might have moved on . . . or got kilt or somethin'. But if it ain't him it don' make no difference: place'll still be the same."

"Yeah." The big man stood up in his stirrups, easing his crotch with his hand. "Well, I reckon we'll look in there. Be nice to have a little whisky, sit on somethin' that ain't movin' all the goddam time." He took up the reins and kneed his horse into a walk. "Any women down there?"

"Useta have a squaw, Indian woman. Cost a buck an' a half. No white women though." The little man followed his boss down the incline.

"White women, Indian squaw, it don't matter to me." They's all the same — with their skirts over their heads," called the tall youngster, riding after them.

"Yeah . . . or a pair o' britches shoved in their faces!" the little man grinned back.

The shacks were a misshapen, lopsided jumble, leaning every which way. Built of logs, assorted planking, and sod walls and patched here and there by stiff buffalo hides, they slumped against each other and held each other up and threatened to pull each other down. There were three altogether, running into each other in a crazy triangle. The space inside the legs of the triangle formed a rough corral where several horses and mules mooned about listlessly. Smoke rose lethargically from a bent chimney and sacking flapped at glassless windows. A bad smell hung over the place.

The riders were fifty yards from the buildings when an orange-coloured mongrel came to meet them, bristling and snarling, and a nasal whine of a voice sang out. "Don' come no further till y'are invited, now!" A second later a shot rang out and lead sang over their heads. "Stay right where y'are and put yuh hands up."

The little man and the youngster looked at the big man. He reined in and nodded to them. "Yeah." He looked amused. "Seems reasonable." They all raised their hands high.

"Welcome to come in," continued the nasal whine. "No guns though. Can give you a little whisky, some grub . . . lil piece of ass, red ass. But you ain't bringin' no weapons in. Okay?"

The three riders exchanged grins. "Sure. Okay," the big man called back. "Obliged to ya." He grinned again at his companions. "Let 'em have the weapons."

"But Pike . . . " the pale youngster began.

"Let 'em have them," said the big man and the youngster shut his mouth.

"Jus' drop yuh guns on the groun'," continued the voice. "An' then come forward one at a time, with yuh hands up. Noah here gonna search yuh, an' if yuh ain't armed yuh can come in. An' don' try nothin' while Noah's doin' the searchin', 'cause I got this rifle on yuh, an' Ah'll shoot. Good at it too. Yuh welcome, long as yuh don' mean no harm."

"Aw, you ain't got nothin' to fear from us, Tobe," called the little man. "Tobe Bleek, ain't it? I been here before. Greeley, Bandy Greeley? Maybe you don' remember?"

"Names don' matter," whined the voice. "Money's what I remember. Come on in now."

The riders dropped their firearms on the ground, came forward one by one, shepherded by the snarling mongrel dog, and were searched by a stocky young man with a sullen expression and suspicious eyes. He took their knives from them and let them pass into the shack then collected the guns and hid them somewhere safe until the new guests would be leaving.

Inside they found an elderly, lean, one-eyed man, incredibly dirty and ragged, leaning on a Kentucky rifle. Two Indian squaws grubbed about, going from one shack to another. A fire burned in a stone fireplace, a rickety table filled the centre of the floor with odd-sized boxes around it for seating. Uneaten food littered the table, old clothes, boots and items of harness littered the floor. The bad smell was worse inside.

"Tobias J. Bleek," the one-eyed man introduced himself. He laid the Kentucky rifle against the wall in a corner. He had a brace of pistols in his belt. "Welcome to Bleek's Place, boys."

"Pike Burden." The big newcomer indicated himself. A little smile of amused tolerance illuminated the dark face. He jerked a thumb towards his two companions. "Bandy Greeley and Joe Kowalski."

Tobe Bleek nodded. "What's your pleasure, boys? Can feed ya — an' yuh horses — an' give yuh a little whisky. Give yuh a bed too — an' yuh don't have to be in it all by yuhself." He nodded to the two squaws. "Fatstuff and Beanpole. Mite homely maybe but haul ashes real good. One thing though: no funny business. I got a brace of pistols here an' me an' Noah there takes turns at guard. Ain't scared to shoot. Hadda do it once or twice already with folks that got too familiar. Like them fellas." He nodded in the direction of the door. Hanging from the roof, just inside the door, were three hanks of hair with rags of shrivelled tissue dangling at the end. Two were dark and greasy, one dirty brown. "Two was Indians," he added by way of explanation.

"Aw, you don't need to worry 'bout us," drawled Burden. "We only lookin' for a rest, some grub an' a little whisky. An' maybe a little fun too." He studied the fat squaw who was fussing at the fire. She had a coarse blanket wrapped round her shapeless, blubbery body and an old duster coat hung over that. Her feet were bare and dirty like the feet of some digging animal. Tiny eyes were almost sunk in the rolls of fat in the round face and thick, dark, greasy hair hung down to her waist. She saw him looking and made a lewd gesture.

"You give smoke? Money?" she grunted.

Burden grimaced. "We're used to better than this," he told Bleek.

"Yeah, but you ain't got much choice right here an' now," returned Bleek confidently. "'Cept for Beanpole. Hey! Beanpole!" he called loudly. "Get yuh red ass in here!"

"Here, Paw." The young man, Noah, appeared from an adjoining shack, holding the second squaw by the arm. She was lean as a rake, her face wrinkled and brown as an elderly monkey's, her hair thin and straggly. She wore an old pair of men's pants. A mangy fur jacket hung over her bare shoulders, revealing the withered breasts. On one foot was a miner's boot stiff with clay, on the other a dilapidated dance slipper.

"Not right now," sighed Burden. "We want to eat first. An' we'll need a little whisky . . . Maybe a lotta whisky, 'fore we tackle that pair."

They fed on stew, fat, greasy and full of gristle, together with sourdough bread and pinto beans. As they ate, the bristly orange dog watched them carefully. Kowalski fed the animal pieces of meat and gristle now and then and even went so far as to rub its head. "Be nice to have a dog," he mused. "Always had a dog at home." He grinned smugly at Greeley. "Paw useta say I hadda way with dogs."

"Yeah. Like your way with women," sneered Greeley.

After they had eaten they settled to an evening's drinking. Later, half-drunk, they tumbled into bad-smelling beds in the adjoining shack, Burden with Fatstuff, Greeley with Beanpole.

"Don' be all goddam night with that squaw," complained the young, pasty Kowalski. "I got a load too, an' I wanna get some sleep between times, so shove her in here when you're through."

"Quit bellyachin'!" called Greeley. "I'm in line afore you. You can have lil Beanpole here when I'm through. Or what's left of her!" There was a crackle of drunken laughter.

In the small hours of the morning Greeley dragged himself outside for a leak and, coming back in, met Burden on his way out. "Stick aroun' for a minute," Burden instructed him. "Wanna talk to ya."

When he returned he had a whisky bottle in his hand. He sat down on the edge of a bed, took a slug, grimaced and handed the bottle to Greeley.

"I been thinkin'," he began. "This ain't such a bad set-up. I mean we could do with a rest for a while. Git tired, ridin' all the time. Be good to hole-up for a spell. Maybe trade a bit, like ol' man Bleek, here; git us a coupla decent squaws, new horses, maybe a bit of white ass from one of them wagon trains now and then." He grinned in friendly lewdness at Greeley. "I don' mean stay here for ever," he assured him. "Few months maybe. See the winter out."

"You mean as partners to ol' man Bleek?" The little man's face had a foxy expression.

"Uh-uh." The big man shook his head. He reached for the bottle and took another slug. "I mean as the new owners."

Greeley considered calmly. "They're on guard alla time," he pointed out. "Young fella's in the main cabin right now, with them pistols and that Kentucky rifle. An' we ain't armed."

"Shit, I don' mean right now." Burden handed the bottle back. "I mean, in the mornin' . . . we pay up an' leave . . . collect our guns. An' come back again later."

"They'll still be on guard," insisted Greeley. "An' there ain't no cover close to the shacks. They'd see us comin', two of them, an' I guess they're pretty good with them guns."

"Yeah, I know all that. But I guess I can figger somethin'. I jus' wanna know how the idea goes down with ya, that's all."

"Suits me. Kinda like the idea of grabbin' a lil piece of the action."

"Okay then." Burden reached for the

bottle and took another slug. "We'll go into the tradin' business. But right now I'm gonna grab me another little piece of red ass. You finished with Skinny Lizzie?"

"Yeah, but Kowalski . . . "

"Aw fug Kowalski! He's jus' the junior partner."

In the morning they ate more of the previous night's greasy stew for breakfast and settled their account with Tobe Bleek. Then, bleary-eyed, foul-smelling and bad-tempered, they rode out.

"You'll find your guns on the ground beside that live oak," Noah Bleek told them. "Knives too. Come again any time, but remember: come with your hands in the air first."

They mounted and rode off, the orange-coloured mongrel following them for a few minutes. Kowalski seemed to think that this fact proved his popularity with dogs. "G'wan home now, boy!" he called to the animal. "You caint come with us. G'wan home now!" He grinned at Burden. "He'd follow me anywhere."

"Yeah?" scowled Burden. "Well, he's about the only . . . Naw! But wait!" He checked his mount momentarily. "Don't send the bastard home. Let him come with us. Okay. You're so goddam good with dogs; get him to follow us. Go on, encourage the bastard."

Kowalski was slow to catch on. "You kiddin'? You really want him? I din't know you liked dogs. What you want a dog for?"

"Never fuggin' mind what I want him for!" growled Burden. "Jus' get the bastard to follow us — go on! Talk to him or somethin' but get him to tag along."

Flattered to be entrusted with such a task, Kowalski spoke to the dog, making encouraging noises of recognition, and the dog followed, tail wagging.

They rode westwards until they were perhaps quarter of a mile from Bleek's Place, then, when the dog appeared to be growing reluctant to follow them much further, Burden turned in his saddle towards Greeley. "You got some thin rope about you?" he enquired. "Some cord?"

"I gotta piece right here, Pike," called Kowalski, anxious to keep in his boss's favour. "Right here in my saddlebag." He fished around behind him for a moment and brought out a coil of light cord.

"Right," grunted Burden. "Git down and put a noose round that fuggin' dog's neck. He's a-comin' with us."

Kowalski was slow again. "You mean you want me to . . . "

"Aw, for Chrissakes!" swore Burden. "Do I havta tell you ever'thin' a dozen fuggin' times? Get down off that horse and tie that fuggin' hound to your saddle. I wanna make sure he comes with us."

"We gonna have a dog?" Kowalski's face lit up with unexpected pleasure. He dismounted and tied the dog by a long line to his saddle horn . . .

Burden smirked at him sardonically.

"Yeah," he said. "We're gonna have a dog. For a little while. Jus' a little while."

Greeley looked at him quizzically. "You thinkin' of . . . ?" He jerked his head backwards in the direction of Bleek's Place.

"Yeah, you got it. But not right now. We'll ride on a-ways . . . wait a while. We'll let them forget about us first."

They rode at a walk until noon then they made camp. They brewed coffee, chewed on some jerky and lay around smoking. The orange mongrel whined and pulled at the rope which tethered him to a tree.

"Don't worry, mutt," leered Burden, "You're goin' home soon — though you ain't maybe goin' to like it."

Kowalski, puzzled, reached into his saddlebag and brought out a bottle of Bleek's whisky. "You want a snort, Pike?" He extended the bottle to his boss.

"Naw. An' you ain't havin' any either. We got work to do. Now listen."

He began to explain his plan. Kowalski looked decidedly unenthusiastic at first but Greeley joshed him along. "So what the hell?" he ragged him. "You can always get another mutt. Country's goddam full of fuggin' mutts."

In mid-afternoon they mounted and rode back the way they had come. They rode at a stealthy walk and when they came within four hundred yards of Bleek's Place they dismounted, concealed by the folds of the land, and went forward on foot, the dog, knowing he was going home, trotting willingly on his rope-leash. They halted in the brush a couple of hundred yards from the shacks. "See anybody aroun'?" Burden asked.

Greeley was studying the shacks from amongst the undergrowth. "Naw," he replied. "Ain't nobody aroun'. They'll be inside mos' likely."

"Good," grinned Burden, "I'll bring 'em out, right smart." He turned to Kowalski. "Now grab that mutt by the noose of the rope an' put a choke hold on him. Don't let the bastard move an inch."

"What you gonna do?" Kowalski seemed uneasy.

"I'm gonna break its fuggin' legs, that's what I'm gonna do," spat Burden. "Now grab hold of the goddam critter."

"Aw, say, Boss," began Kowalski, "you ain't . . . I mean you ain't gonna . . . "

Greeley, the little man, looked round in amusement. "Listen to him," he laughed quietly. "He's shot the guts out of a man without turnin' a hair; he's listened to the screams of a woman that he's rapin' an' only enjoyed it all the more. An' now he's goin' soft on us over a goddam mutt."

Burden was less amused. "Look, ya dumb bastard," he ridiculed Kowalski, "this is a mutt, a worthless goddam mongrel. They're as common as rats. You gonna worry 'bout a goddam mutt when there's nice little pickin's here for all of us? Doncha like the idea of a nice lil place of our own? We can have a nice comfortable place here for the winter . . . get some new squaws . . . maybe get yourself a lil piece of white ass offa one of them wagon trains. No more hard ridin' for a while. Jus' lie aroun' all day. We can do all that — but we got to get them bastards outa that cabin. I think this is the way to do it. Now will ya hold that goddam mutt? Bandy, you keep an eye on the shack."

Kowalski paused for a moment in puzzled thought then his face split into a grin. His delinquent mind did a grotesque somersault, untypical growing tenderness giving way to habitual callousness and cruelty. "Yeah, what the hell!" he chuckled. "Ever'thin' got to die sometime. Come here, ya ugly yaller bastard!" He seized the rope and tightened it suddenly to the point where the dog could hardly breathe. The animal struggled furiously, terrified and gasping.

"Hold it! Hold it tight!" grunted

Burden in annoyance. He grabbed a jerking hind leg and wrenched it savagely. A strangled howl tore the air. "I tol' ya to keep the bastard quiet!" he swore at Kowalski. "Now hol' him tight." He was half-kneeling now, one knee on the leaping body of the thrashing dog. He positioned his hands carefully on the damaged leg and bent it savagely with all his strength. There was an audible snap and a yelping wail of anguish from the wretched animal and the trapped body leapt and writhed frantically. "Can't you keep the bastard quiet?" he grunted hoarsely at Kowalski. "We don't want too much noise . . . yet. Now where's that other goddam laig?" He grabbed the second hind leg and broke it like a rotten stick. This time only a gasping squeak could be heard. "Now we're gonna put him out there where Mister Bleek or his boy Noah can fin' him. Okay. You can let him go now. Let him make all the noise he wants, more the better. Put him out there in the clear then get back here an' take cover."

"Wait!" Kowalski was thinking. "You put him out there like this an' he can still get to the shack. Dogs can crawl . . . draggin' their hind parts."

Burden paused. "Yeah, well . . . "

"You hold him." Kowalski handed him the rope. "Watch he don't bite ya. Keep him nearly fuggin' strangled." And as Burden choked off the animal's air supply Kowalski seized the front legs, one at a time, and, wrenching and straining, tore the tendons. "He won't go far now," he grinned. "We can put him out to be found. He'll howl plenty, too."

They threw the howling animal bodily through the air and out of the brush to lie squirming in the open and withdrew further into cover.

"Now get your guns out," Burden told them. "Ol' Toby Bleek gonna come out when he hears that mutt howlin', or his boy Noah is . . . an' we gotta be ready for 'em."

It didn't take long. In minutes, Noah Bleek emerged from the shack, a Kentucky rifle in his hands. He walked slowly in the direction of the noise then stopped warily. "Flash?" he called. "You there boy? Come on Flash!" Toby Bleek too came out of the shack and followed his son, his two pistols in his hands. They advanced slowly, suspiciously, their eyes taking in the country around them.

Noah Bleek whistled and walked forward a few yards at a time. "Come on Flash boy!" he called, his voice warm and encouraging.

"Take it easy, son." Bleek senior warned him. "Could be a goddam trap. Maybe goddam Indians . . . or them fellas that was here last night . . . "

"But that's ol' Flash," protested Noah, reluctant to ignore the pitiful howls. "I'm goddam sure of it. An' where did he git to anyways? We ain't seen him all day. He wouldn't go off like that, on his own. Somethin's happened."

"Yeah . . . well, it could be a trap. Like you say, it ain't like ol' Flash to git in trouble . . . an' it ain't no use us gittin' killed over a . . . Look! Over there!" He pointed to the writhing body on the ground.

Noah was running forward. "Naw!" called his father. "Don't go no further! Could be a trap!" Noah stopped, irresolute.

"Come on, Noah boy," murmured Burden, sighting on him from the brush. "Jus' a little bit further, so's I can be sure."

"You take the boy," Greeley whispered hoarsely. "Kowalski an' me'll take the ol' man."

"It's Flash all right!" called Noah to his father. "Hurt, too . . . bad . . . can't walk . . . can't even git up." He started forward again, a few careful steps, and there was the roar of a rifle and he jerked violently to the side and collapsed in a heap. Toby Bleek was suddenly running back towards the shack, his stiff old legs working like rusty pistons. There was another shot but he kept going.

Greeley and Kowalski broke from the brush and were tearing after him, speedily reducing the distance between them. Both of them had pistols and one fired. Toby Bleek stumbled, recovered, turned and fired both pistols in frantic succession then hobbled fearfully on.

They caught him just as he reached the door, falling on him like hounds on a wounded deer. They began clubbing him with their pistols. Incredibly, the door opened and Beanpole, the thin squaw, rushed out in a fearful fury, a knife in her hands. She didn't hesitate but flung herself on the two men, swearing and spitting. Kowalski shoved his pistol close to the skinny body and blasted the life out of her. Greeley cut Toby Bleek's throat.

When Burden came up it was all over. He stood for a moment, looking down and nodding satisfactorily. "Hadda kill one of the squaws, huh?" he observed. "Well, we still got the best one." He went into the shack and found the fat squaw cowering trembling in a corner. He went up to her and grabbed her by the chin, holding her in a vice-like grip. "They're all dead out there, Baby," he told her, grinning wickedly. "But you're still alive . . . an' you get to stay that way, long as you behave. So don't get no ideas 'bout runnin' away, see?" He shoved her away and walked to the door, then called back to her over his shoulder. "You got the work of two women to do aroun' here now."

5

DEATH, once again, did not come for him. He lay in his miserable corner for thirty hours and woke up with his bladder nearly bursting, his mouth and throat parched and his leg swollen like a balloon.

He did not know whether he was glad or sorry to re-awaken. He stirred, and a hundred aches and pains racked his weary body. Dragging himself out to relieve himself was torture and the process took him nearly an hour. He drank all the water in his canteen, wanted more, but could not make the effort to drag himself to the creek. He crawled back into his shelter and sought oblivion in sleep again.

Several times during the next few days he woke up and considered, yet again, whether he should end the whole sorry business. Laboriously, he loaded the rifle — he could not find the pistol anywhere — then lay looking at it and wondering whether, if he tried again to shoot himself, his arms and hands might work this time. But he did not try it. At one point a strange thought crossed his mind: If he *did* shoot himself, who would be there to defend him when those Indians returned? In spite of his suffering he grinned at the absurdity of the idea, and that grin was the turning point for him. A man may not value his life when it isn't in danger, but when he has had to struggle fiercely to keep it he often becomes very reluctant to let it go. Joe Bradley knew how near he had been to death — every move he made reminded him of that — and something deep inside him made him hang on to life. He wasn't going to throw away something that he had fought so hard and suffered so much to defend.

So he faced up to life again. After a couple of days he dragged himself to the creek, bagged himself with water and filled his canteen. Back in his shelter he filled his mouth with raw cornmeal and chewed slowly. Now and then he struggled to get out what was left of the side of bacon. He could not cut it or cook it and contented himself by chewing the edge of the raw meat.

He was afraid to look at his leg. It had swelled to three times its normal size and throbbed frighteningly. He could feel no sensation in his lower leg or in his foot and had to drag the limb behind him when he crawled. Each time he dragged himself to the creek he soaked the shirt-bandage that enclosed the wound but otherwise he was too unsure and too afraid to touch it. What would happen if gangrene set in and the leg went rotten? He simply daren't think of that.

He had other injuries too and he gave his attention to those. After a few days he could see out of the eye that had been closed. True, he could only partly see because a great shadow closed off half his vision, but still, that was an improvement. The bloody groove in his neck and scalp throbbed excruciatingly, his neck was stiff to the point of rigidity and flies encrusted the wound during the daylight hours. He took a little sack that had once contained shot, soaked it in the creek and tied it round his neck as the best and only treatment available. The deep scrape on his rib-cage quickly scabbed over and began to heal cleanly.

Slowly he began to recover. He was young, had a good constitution and, most important, had the desire to hold on to life. In a couple of weeks he could hobble painfully and was cooking food and eating voraciously. The great swelling on his leg began to go down and he felt some slight sensation coming back into his foot. One day he felt sufficiently optimistic to unwind the shirt-bandage. What he saw almost stopped his heart: the leg was fiery-red and purple and a great scab stood an inch proud over the place where the gap had been; when he cautiously unwound the rope that he had bound round it the deep grooves remained in the flesh, making the limb look like a joint of raw meat, trussed and ready for the oven.

He gently pressed his forefinger into the swollen flesh and was relieved to see it spring back from the depression. It didn't look as if it was infected. His spirits rose another point or two.

As soon as he was able he saw to his horses and found three more Indian ponies grazing with them. He transferred his saddle to one of the ponies and, his rifle slung over his shoulders, rode gently back to the scene of the latest battle. He had to find the pistol.

A flock of buzzards took to the air as he approached the scene and there was a scurrying of coyotes or other scavengers. A roaring of flies filled the air and he had to steel himself to go on.

Nobody could have mistaken the

place for anything but a battlefield. The broken bodies, the trampled and churned earth and litter of weapons strewn around shouted out loudly of violence, wounding and death. He checked his pony and sat there, dazed and bemused, wondering how he could have survived such destruction. Then the thought came to him that it was *his* battlefield; he was the victor; most of the violence had been his. That stupefied him even further.

Eventually he slid off the pony and began searching for the pistol. He found it, but not until he had turned over one or two of the dead bodies, a gruesome task. There were other weapons too — several lances, two bows, another stone axe and a rough buffalo-hide quiver with half-a-dozen arrows in it. He stuck the pistol in his belt, tied the other weapons together with some rawhide and took them all back to his shelter.

That evening, as he sat over a tiny fire eating supper, he was forced to reconsider himself and his life again. Those dead men, lying back there, he had killed them. Him. Joe Bradley. He had fought other men for his life and he had won. He had taken their lives instead. More Indians would come for him, that was certain. He would have to fight like that again, kill more men — or perhaps be killed himself.

He looked inside himself to find out if he was afraid and found, again, that he was not. If he had to fight again he would, just as he had that last time. If he was killed . . . well, that would just have to happen: he couldn't do much about being dead. But he would fight like all hell to save his life, and he wasn't afraid to do it.

The thought overwhelmed him. He wasn't afraid! And suddenly he realized that, until he had come out into this savage land, he *had* been afraid, had lived all his life in fear. He hadn't been a fighting man, ever. And it hadn't been because he was wiser or more compassionate than other men — as he'd liked to pretend to himself: it had been because he had been afraid of violence. He knew that now with an undeniable certainty.

But that was no longer the case. He'd been given no choice in whether or not he would fight: he'd had battle thrust upon him and had had no alternative but either to fight or die. He hadn't had time to be afraid. And something in him, the man he really was under the protective fear, had fought to stay alive. Now, for him, fear was redundant.

A grim, serious but strangely comforting thought filled his mind: he had come out to this fierce wilderness to *surrender* his life . . . and instead, he had *found* it — a real, full life . . . not the half-hearted version he had lived up till now.

He shook his head slowly in puzzlement as he gulped his cooling coffee. What would happen to him now, he wondered. He didn't know . . . but he was ready to face it, whatever it might be. And he knew that the emotional scars which he had carried since the deaths of his wife and son were — however slowly — beginning to heal.

He woke next morning in a positive frame of mind. He'd have to get better quickly. Those red bastards would come again. And he didn't have all the powder and shot in the world. Better conserve it as much as possible. Could he use some of the captured weapons? He tried the bows and arrows. The bows were stout, rough weapons, made from some kind of thick branch, bound and strung with animal sinew and damned hard to draw. The arrows were mixed, some with flint heads, some simply hardened and barbed at the point. He tried his hand at shooting at a target and wasn't surprised to get poor results. "Well, it figgers," he consoled himself. "But I'll keep practisin'. Maybe have need of it sometime . . . an' right now I still got a gun."

* * *

The band of Shoshone braves sat round the fire uneasily. Bloody Hand was haranguing them again. What kind of men were they? The light-skinned man was on his own! He was only one! True, he had guns — but guns could only be made to work once, then he had to have a long time to prepare them to work again. And there had been many Shoshone braves. Braves? He spat out the word. They had been afraid! That was the explanation. Let them admit it. They had acted like women. If they had attacked wholeheartedly they could have battered him to the ground, run him through with their lances. Bloody Hand swung an imaginary axe and fiercely stabbed an imaginary opponent as he thought of it. If he, Bloody Hand, had had the use of his two hands . . .

Wolfskin interrupted him angrily. Bloody Hand was wrong. Bloody Hand had not been close to the lone whiteskin . . . had not seen the fearless ferocity of him. Truly, that man could not be killed. He had wonderful charms about him. Had he not fought their whole band? Killed four of them and wounded one more?

Several other braves joined in vehemently. Wolfskin was right! The whiteskin was not an ordinary man. Three-Pawed Bear had run him through the leg with his lance — and he hadn't even noticed it! Surely that was great medicine? Cougar-Heart had clubbed him several times to the head — and still he had battled, absolutely without fear. Man-Burner and Knife-in-the-Belly and all the others, they had attacked him — fiercely — all of them — at the same time! Any other man would have crumpled before them. But that man . . . he was not an ordinary man . . . He was truly a great warrior. They did not like the idea of another attack on him.

Bloody Hand spat in disgust. They were women! They had been frightened by the whiteskin's ferocity. But he,

Bloody Hand, was not afraid. He was a killer too. Just wait till he had the use of his two hands, had recovered from his wounds. He would go to another Shoshone village, raise another band. They would try the whiteskin again. And next time it would be different.

* * *

He drew the bow back, held the arrow at his ear for a second and let fly. There was the 'whorr' of the bowstring, a whisper of air as the arrow sped forward and the soft 'thut' as the barbed point pierced the straw target which he had rigged up. Bradley lowered the bow, unimpressed. Sure, he had hit the target — but it had taken him four shots to do it, and the range was only about forty yards. He'd have to do a lot better than that if he was ever going to hunt with the bow.

He walked to the target and collected the fallen arrows. *Hunting*. Seemed like a good idea. He'd used up all of the bacon during his period of recovery, and there wasn't a lot of flour or cornmeal left either. He'd have to go hunting soon . . . but he was reluctant to use powder and shot. He'd need all of that if — no, not *if* but, *when* — those Indians attacked again.

Was he fit to go hunting now? He flexed his bad leg. It didn't hurt too much. Sure, he walked with a bit of a limp, but that would maybe stay with him for the rest of his life now. His ribs were totally healed and the deep gouge in his neck and scalp was covered with painless scab. He could move his neck almost normally and he could see out of both eyes. Yeah, he was fit enough to go hunting. Could he use the bow well enough? Well, hunting would give him keen practice . . . and he could take the rifle along just in case. The truth was he was frustrated by being confined to a small area for a lengthy period of time and wanted movement and action. He went and saddled one of the captured Indian ponies, put the pack-saddle on another, loaded the Springfield, provided himself with powder and shot and rode out in the late morning.

He rode slowly and carefully, looking for tracks, tracks of animals and tracks of men, and keeping a sharp lookout all around him. He saw occasional elk tracks but no elk. He saw prairie chickens and, twice, wild turkey, but they were too far away for the bow and he didn't want to use the gun.

He rode further than he realized and in mid-afternoon, feeling hungry, he dismounted by a little creek and made the best kind of meal he could out of some uncooked cornmeal washed down with water. He was resting his leg, chewing cornmeal, when he saw the movement amongst the trees fifty yards away. He stretched out slowly, belly to the ground, and strained his eyes in that direction. What was it? Animal or human? He reached out very slowly and brought the Springfield up alongside him.

There it was again! Just the faintest flicker of movement. Almost invisible, whatever it was. He found he was hardly breathing, his heart beating fast. Was he going to have to fight again?

He saw an antelope's head, clear and plain for a brief second through the branches of the intervening trees. His excitement hardly eased. Antelope was meat, and the idea of meat was particularly inviting after weeks of only flour and cornmeal. Would it come nearer? Dare he go after it? Was anyone else stalking it? He lay still and watched.

The antelope was moving in his direction, grazing in fits and starts, raising its head and scenting the wind every few seconds. He'd been lucky . . . hadn't had to stalk it . . . it had come to him. If only it kept coming. He reached stealthily for the bow. Dare he try a shot?

It was moving away now, completely unaware of his presence. Moving further away . . . still grazing, still scenting the air. He could see the beautiful coat, the delicate colours. Where there was one there might be others.

But it was getting further and further away, moving towards a little canyon thickly clothed with pine wood. If it went in there he could maybe trap it? Box it in? He watched it make its way into the canyon, grazing, sniffing the air, looking all around.

He lay still and let it disappear and waited ten more minutes. Then he rose and slipped off his boots. He slung the quiver of arrows over his shoulder, took the bow in one hand and the rifle in the other and began to follow the animal.

He moved with great care, testing every step before he took it. As far as he could tell the wind was in his favour. With luck he'd have antelope steak tonight for dinner. He found his mouth was watering.

It was ahead of him. He could see it plainly, fifty yards away, browsing on some low bushes. He waited for it to move on and as he did so he saw its head come up, its ears pricked high. Had it scented him? Or heard him? It moved a few nervous paces, took a little bound. He saw that it could get out of the canyon by scampering over the top edge. It paused again, sniffing the breeze.

It would have to be the rifle. Otherwise he was going to lose it. Quietly he set the bow down, raised the Springfield and sighted. No time to dally. He squeezed the trigger and saw it jump. Once only. Convulsively. A low jerk, really. As the sound boomed through the canyon he knew that the antelope was his.

It was still breathing when he reached it. He cut its throat and let it bleed dry then heaved it across his shoulders. He carried it back towards the place where he had rested by the creek earlier. As he emerged from the trees he stopped abruptly.

Indians! A large number of them, silently examining his ponies. They saw him coming and froze, staring at him.

He stopped too, staring back at them.

He couldn't move — certainly not quickly, being barefoot and with an antelope across his shoulders. And he hadn't reloaded the rifle. He remained standing still. He didn't know what to do.

The Indians didn't move either. Now that he had time to observe them he saw that they weren't all men: some were boys, young boys. Further back from them he could see more Indians . . . some of them looked like women . . . Jesus! Was the whole Indian nation gathering here?

The nearest ones were trying to talk to him, gesticulating. Why hadn't they attacked? They seemed peaceful. Another man was riding up towards them from the mass at the back. He had no feathers in his hair and wore a kind of deerskin tunic. Bradley heaved the antelope off his shoulders and on to the ground. What was going to happen now? Where had these Indians come from? Why hadn't he heard them coming? The ones round the ponies were muttering excitedly.

"'Allo! 'Allo! Is all right. You have the fine antelope, oui? Maybe you share him with us, heh? We give you something. Is all right. You no need gun."

He couldn't believe it. The man on the dun pony was talking to him. Talking to him in English.

"These ponies . . . you take them from the Shoshone? From Bloody Hand, no?" The deerskin-clad man slid from his horse and gestured towards Bradley's Indian ponies. One still bore the red hand on its rump.

"Is all right." The deerskin man held up his hand reassuringly. Bradley realized that he had unconsciously raised the Springfield and was holding it like a club.

"You speak English?" The words stuck in his throat. How long was it since he had spoken to anyone? "Who are you? Where have all these Indians . . . "

"Oui. I speak the English . . . a little . . . Louis Deveraux." He jerked a thumb towards himself. "From Canada. But living now with the Sioux. I have Sioux woman."

"Are these Indians safe? They won't attack?" Still the words stuck in his throat. He seemed to be dreaming.

"Non, non. They no attack. Not you . . . not now, anyway. They know about you. You fight the Shoshone braves. Take Shoshone ponies and scalps, oui?"

"The Shoshone? You mean Shoshone Indians? Ain't these Shoshone Indians then?" He gestured to the many Indians surrounding them.

"Non. Non. These the Sioux. Enemies of Shoshone. We hear how you fight Shoshone. Kill many."

Bradley was shaking Deveraux by the hand, still in a daze. "Where are you from? Where are you going? How come you all happen to be here?"

"I tell you. Louis Deveraux. From Canada. Long time ago. I trade with

Sioux for furs, buffalo robes. But now I stay with Sioux, for little while anyway. Maybe go back to Canada one day." The French-Canadian gestured towards the muttering Indians. "This whole Sioux village. Moving to better grazing and hunting ground. We hear shot. Boom! Boom! Then find ponies. We recognize Shoshone ponies by markings. Bloody Hand. All know of Bloody Hand. You want trade ponies? Sioux give plenty for Shoshone ponies. Plenty-plenty for Bloody Hand pony."

"Eh . . . I don' know . . . " All he wanted to do, strangely, was get out of there. The nearness of his escape and the presence of so many Indians unnerved him. "Naw. I don' want to trade. Not right now."

"Is fine antelope you have, oui? You give me piece of him. I give you powder . . . shot too. How you say, heh?" Deveraux was grinning, openly friendly. The idea of powder and shot was attractive to Bradley.

"Well . . . maybe . . . if that's what

you want. Say, how come you got powder an' shot to spare, out here?"

"Oh. I ride to fort. Fort Laramie. Some time I go. Bring furs there. Bring back powder, shot, whisky, meal. You trade half of antelope?"

"Yeah . . . well, okay . . . "

"Shielle! Shielle!" Deveraux called over his shoulder and beckoned to someone in the crowd of Indians at his back. "Come. Cut up carcase. Toute suite!" He indicated the antelope on the ground and began untying two deerskin bags from behind his saddle.

There was movement among the crowd of watching Indian women. A young woman came forward and stood looking at Deveraux. He drew a knife from his belt and handed it to her. She knelt down and began expertly to draw the carcase. That done, she set about butchering it.

Bradley watched, still highly uneasy. The girl's arms were bloody to the elbows. She was brown-skinned and her features were good; clear dark eyes and white teeth. When she bent over her task Bradley could not help noticing her rump; generous, round and smooth. As she straightened up he caught a glimpse of her bosom; two gently-swelling brown globes pushing out her deerskin tunic.

Deveraux was measuring out powder and shot into a deerskin bag. He held it out to Bradley. "You sure you no want to trade Bloody Hand pony? They give you plenty furs. Good furs."

"Naw. Not right now. Maybe later." Bradley had had enough of surprise for one day. He wanted to get away. He wanted to be by himself. To think. He found himself loading the new meat on to his pack-pony, helped by the young woman, Shielle.

He mounted and took up the lead-rein of the pack-pony. "I'll look for you, another time," he called to Deveraux. "Talk some more. Glad to have met ya." He dug his pony in the ribs with his heels then reined in again. "That your Indian woman?" He indicated the bloody-armed Shielle.

"Non." Deveraux laughed. "My woman Sioux. Shielle Arapahoe woman. Captured by Sioux. She only worker. How you say . . . Slave? Au'voir mon ami. I see you other time. You want to find Sioux village, you follow trail-sign. Is easy. Au'voir!"

6

BRADLEY stepped back and studied his handiwork. The last wall of the cabin was complete, tidy and strong. True, there was no door, just the opening for a door, but he could hang a blanket there. That would keep out draughts until he could cut enough wood for a door. He went inside the cabin. The fireplace he had built — a rock base filled with earth — would ensure warmth and decent cooking. A hole in the roof let the smoke out and another rough square hole in one wall, a crude window, let light in. He'd rig up a shutter of some kind to fix over that in bad weather. In addition there were loopholes in each wall that he could shoot through in case of a siege. Taken all round, it wasn't bad. Sure, he could build a better cabin, given time, but this would do for now . . . would have to do.

He glanced at the rough bed-framework that stood in one corner, light branches tied with rawhide. He didn't have much in the way of bedding . . . maybe he could get some furs or buffalo robes from those Sioux Indians? That'd be soft and warm . . . He felt the stiffening in his groin again as he thought of that and marvelled that he could feel that way after all he had been through. But that was healthy; he was feeling positive; he was *living*.

He laid the axe in a corner and went outside to where his horses grazed. There were eight of them now, his own two and six Indian ponies. How many should he take? And which ones? What if they wouldn't deal? He didn't like to think of that. They had to deal. He'd take the Bloody Hand pony, for one. They seemed to think highly of that one — probably because it had belonged to Bloody Hand.

He finally made his choice, four of them, the first two he had acquired and two of the most recent. He tied them together in two pairs with their hackamores then saddled his own horse, mounted and rode out, leading them behind him.

He didn't have any difficulty finding the Sioux trail. The ground had been trampled as though a herd of buffalo had passed that way and there were many grooves in the earth made by their travois. He followed it for two days and knew he was approaching it when it was still half a mile away by the smoke from the many cooking fires.

That didn't prevent him from being caught.

Riding along, at a slow walk and making plenty of noise to announce his arrival, he turned a bend in the trail and found himself facing three Indians with drawn bows. He reined in immediately and held up one hand, palm forward. He felt decidedly foolish. Was the gesture ridiculous? Or did it mean anything to Indians? He heard sounds behind him and saw, out of the corner of his eye, two more Indians coming up at his back. Well, he had come looking for them and he had found them. He hoped it would be all right.

"Deveraux," he said, trying to keep his voice calm. "Deveraux. Louis Deveraux. My friend." He touched his chest with his hand.

A lance point was an inch from his belly. Two Indians were studying the Bloody Hand pony with great interest. After a few minutes one took his horse by the bridle and then they were making their way towards the Indian village, a little cavalcade of them, him in front, being led. An Indian followed right at his back, lance at the ready, and two more followed, leading his ponies.

He saw a wide clearing scattered with tall tepees. A dozen dogs ran to meet them, barking and snarling, and fell in alongside them. There was considerable smoke, the smell of cooking, ponies grazing everywhere and lots of people moving around. A stronger smell assailed his nostrils from time to time, a bad smell, but he preferred not to think what it might be.

He was standing amongst a small group of Indian men, unable to talk to them and feeling decidedly uneasy. Several other braves were examining his ponies with great interest. He hoped they didn't get too keen on them. Women were coming and going, doing their daily tasks, but there was no sign of the woman Shielle and no sign of Deveraux. What if Deveraux wasn't there? Maybe he had gone back to Canada. What the hell would he do if . . . ?

Several men were coming towards him and he saw Deveraux among them. He breathed a sigh of relief. Thank God!

"Eh, mon ami!" Deveraux seemed glad enough to see him. "You bring the ponies, oui? You need the powder and shot? C'est bien, c'est bien. We give. Maybe you like to trade the gun also, oui? They give you plenty for the gun. Plenty furs, robes, meat also. What you say, eh? But you stay eat with us anyway, heh? Is long time I no speak with Yankee." He turned to the braves examining the ponies and made some guttural sounds. The braves stepped back a little although they still eyed the ponies with great interest.

"Well, it ain't quite that." Now that he came to it Bradley found it difficult to get it out. "I got powder an' shot . . . not a lot, but enough to get by . . . "

"Ah! You want furs? The beaver, fox, we have. Also buffalo robes. Is good."

"Yeah, well . . . " It was goddam awkward. The words were sticking in his throat. To make it worse his groin was stiffening again — just the thing he hoped wouldn't happen. Deveraux and the braves were looking at him, waiting.

"Yeah, sure I could do with some

furs, but I was thinking . . . "

Deveraux had sensed the awkwardness. He was looking at him curiously. A ghost of a smile began to form round the French-Canadian's lips. "There is maybe something else, non?"

"Hell, I'll tell you what it is . . . " He decided to blurt it out in any way he could, get it over with. "I need a woman — Naw! not just that way — I mean to cook, and stuff like that. An' I was wonderin' 'bout that captive Arapahoe woman . . . Shielle . . .is that her name?" He knew very well that that was her name. "I mean, do you think . . . Would it be possible . . . Don't get me wrong . . . I mean, who does she belong . . . Aw shit!" He stopped in confusion, feeling wretched and miserable.

"Mmmmmmmm." Deveraux was stroking his chin, thinking. There was a long pause, and when he spoke again his voice was low and uncertain. "If she was a Sioux woman . . . No, no, they would not. But she is a captive, like a captured pony. Well, we can see The Old Crow. She will have little use for ponies, but she can exchange them for other things."

"The Old Crow?" Bradley's hopes rose slightly.

"Oui. Shielle was captured from her own people by The Panther, The Old Crow's son, but The Panther is dead. Three month ago a horse fall, roll on him. So Shielle work for The Old Crow now. Sometimes for other people too, but we see The Old Crow. Maybe she . . . Come! We go."

Everybody seemed to know now what was happening. A considerable crowd of Indians, not all of them men, were hurrying along beside them through the camp. They stared at Bradley with great interest and muttered amongst themselves. Some of the squaws were laughing openly. Bradley's face burned. He felt like making a break for it but it was too late now. Besides, he was determined to see the thing through.

The Old Crow had been forewarned of their coming. She was sitting in state before her tepee, a shrivelled hag of around sixty, smoking a long pipe. The girl Shielle was doing something inside the tepee. She kept glancing out, curious, apprehensive glances.

Deveraux spoke to the old woman while the crowd hung on his every word. He drew her attention to Bradley's ponies, which the braves had brought along, paying particular attention to the one with the red hand on its rump. From time to time he brought some of the braves into the conversation as if to confirm his own claims. The braves seemed enthusiastic.

The old squaw began talking and went on and on in a cracked, guttural voice, making many gestures and occasionally wailing out loud. She stopped at one point and dragged the girl Shielle out of the tepee then resumed her monologue. The girl glanced up at Bradley from under lowered brows; frightened, worried glances. Bradley could only gesture, slightly and gently, and try to look kind.

Finally Deveraux turned back to Bradley. “She take all four ponies and the gun and whisky. Then she let Shielle go.” There was a loud murmur from the crowd and they watched Bradley with great interest.

Bradley shook his head. “I only trade three ponies. Red Hand pony and two others. Other one I trade for furs. And I don’t trade the gun. No way. Pity.” He shrugged his shoulders and made as if to move off.

The Old Crow broke out into a wail, followed by a long guttural diatribe. At the end there was a sound from the watching crowd that was very like laughter, but cruel, sardonic laughter. Bradley waited for Deveraux to translate.

“She say the girl very valuable. Ver’ good worker. Cook, sew, make buffalo robe, moccasins — an’ keep bed very warm.”

Bradley shook his head. "Naw. No deal. Tell her I go back east, or Fort Laramie maybe. Find a woman from one of the wagon trains. I'll trade the three ponies to the braves for furs." He moved towards the ponies and took hold of the Bloody Hand one by the forelock to lead it away.

The Old Crow broke out into a desperate wailing, holding her hands high and shaking her head. Deveraux called out, grinning: "She says she'll take the three ponies — and that knife." He indicated the sharpened, domestic knife that Bradley had taken from the Shoshone brave.

"Naw." Bradley knew the value of that knife. "Jus' the three ponies. Red Hand one's a good one: brave will give her a lot for that." He paused a moment. There was no response. He began to lead his ponies away.

There was a babble of guttural sounds. "Oui! Ca va! Ca ca!" Deveraux broke in hurriedly. "She say is okay. She take three pony. She say take girl away. Girl is lazy woman-dog. Take her away quick!"

The old squaw had pushed the girl Shielle towards Bradley and was berating her, scolding her, as if the girl had been in some way to blame. The girl was bewildered, frightened. She looked from Deveraux to Bradley and back to the old squaw. The old squaw jabbered at her, spitting and cursing. Deveraux spoke quietly to the girl. She stood silent, looking at Bradley with wide, frightened eyes. Bradley smiled at her, looking as gentle as he could, then stepped forward and took her by the arm. She resisted for a moment, her arm warm in his hand, then, with her head held low and her face averted, she went with him.

* * *

The first night back at his cabin, Bradley gave the girl the bed.

"For you," he told her, showing her the bed-frame and handing her a blanket and several beaver pelts. "Keep warm. Sleep." He wrapped a pelt round his neck and snuggled into it, miming warmth, and then mimed sleep. The girl watched him nervously. It was obvious that she was unhappy and afraid. Bradley hung a blanket over the open doorway and went out and left her to it.

He himself slept with his horses. With two Indian ponies there, besides his own two animals, there was a chance that she might run away, and he didn't want that. So he tethered the four animals to one picket rope, spread a blanket on the ground, and with his saddle for a pillow kept a sleepy guard over them. Besides, he had other reasons for leaving her alone.

The first few days with her were very tense and awkward. She spoke no English and he knew nothing of her language and though he wanted to quieten her fears and reassure her he could do little to effect this. She watched him almost continuously, her eyes big with fright as though she expected violence from him. What she thought he expected from her was difficult to figure out, for during the days she simply stayed in the cabin till he called her and then sat around the fire, watching him with her big, frightened eyes and clearly not knowing what to do.

In all his life before, Bradley had only known one woman, his wife, and he'd never been the great lover. Fact was, he'd been a boy when he'd first got married and afterwards his time and energy had been pretty well consumed by hard-labour farming; he'd had little chance to develop sexual or social skills. But he was a different man now, with a different outlook on a lot of things.

He began by speaking to her a lot, in English, the only language he knew. From his work with horses he knew that it was not only the words used but the tone of voice that mattered, so he spoke quietly and patiently to her, repeating words over and over again and making accompanying gestures.

"Corn — Meal — Mush," he pronounced, holding the tin pan out to her in one hand while he held the spoon in the other. "Food." He took a spoonful, carried it to his mouth and swallowed. "Good." He put on a ridiculously pleased expression. "You eat." He offered her the spoon. She took it without enthusiasm and spooned some mush into her mouth. "Good?" Bradley made the word a question.

"Good." She gave him the word back with a descending intonation. It was an answer. The first communication had been established.

Nevertheless, though he longed to possess her, Bradley knew that for their partnership to be a successful and lasting one the physical act had to please and satisfy both parties and that meant patience, and so for many long chilly nights he continued to sleep on the ground beside his horses.

During the days he demonstrated

his cooking to her, preparing cornmeal mush and baking primitive bread-cakes on hot stones from the little flour he had left. She watched him carefully but uncertainly, as though she was unsure whether she was permitted to participate in this ritual, but one day he brought in two rabbits that he had snared and the deadlock was broken. She saw him begin to skin the animals and shook her head emphatically at him, holding out her hands for the rabbits and the knife. He handed everything over to her and in a few minutes she had the job done. She pointed to the tin pan, a questioning look on her face. Bradley nodded enthusiastically. In a few minutes more she had the meat cut into pieces and lying in water in the pan.

"Good! Good! You're very clever!" Bradley beamed at her and patted her on the arm. Another stage of their relationship had been completed: it was the first time he had touched her.

Other things too they learned from

each other. She watched him washing at the creek every morning and shyly began to follow his example. One morning, after an insufficient breakfast of mush, she drew a rough drawing of a buffalo in the dusty earth then pointed to him and to the rifle. Gradually, awkwardly, she made him understand that he was to take her with him on the hunt. They set out together, with her mounted on one of the Indian ponies and the pack horse in tow. They killed a lone bull — a cow would have been even better — which he skinned and she butchered with great expertise. That night they dined royally on thick stew along with wild potatoes and wild onions that she had gathered.

The summer was fading, the evenings getting colder. There was a sequence of four nights when a chill rain fell and Bradley was forced to take shelter inside the cabin. She watched him anxiously as he settled, wrapped in his blanket, just inside the doorway, but appeared quickly to accept his presence.

Later, there was a night when wolves howled away off in the dark and she sat up in bed wide-eyed and uneasy. He went to her then and sat with her and talked to her and put his arm around her. She clung to him, her firm shapely body warm against him, and soon he was holding her and caressing her, but gently, gradually, letting her set the pace. Though he hadn't ever been a ladies' man, Bradley sensed from her reactions that she was a virgin. Later, when he found his shuddering release in her he knew by her ecstatic jerks and hoarse gasping that she too had found fulfilment, and later still, when she lay in his arms, happy and content, he knew in his heart that she was his. She was a woman now, as he was a man, and they had a full, positive, adult partnership. They could achieve a lot together, even in this fierce, wild country.

7

THE axe swung and chopped, swung and chopped and in a few minutes the last of the latest batch of young trees was trimmed to a long, clean pole. Bradley tied the load together and hitched it to his pack horse. Another few days of this and he would have enough for a small corral. That would be better. Keep his horses together, instead of wandering all over the place. Safer, too.

He straightened his gently-aching back. He ought to get a dog. Should have got one from those Sioux Indians. Dog would give good warning of anybody coming. Be good for Shielle, too, company for her when he was away.

He moved to take the horse's head then paused to look around him at the space he had cleared. This was a good place, he decided, taking it all in. He'd chosen better than he knew, that night when he'd decided to make a stand here. There was good water close by, and timber for building. Little further out there was great grassland. Cattle would do well here . . . grow fat for nothing on that endless grass. And it wouldn't always be a wilderness. Wagon trains were already beginning to come through, going all the way to Oregon and California. In a few years people were going to settle on this land. There'd be towns and villages all over this area. But he was here now, one of the very first. By the time them folks got here he could be well established, have a cattle ranch — a goddam *big* cattle ranch — all set up.

He began to lead the horse-drawn load back in the direction of the cabin. Building a ranch wouldn't be easy though. No sense kidding himself about that. He'd have to fight. Again and again. Those Shoshone Indians wouldn't give up easily. And what about the Sioux? They were friendly enough right now, but could you be sure they'd always be that way? And if he did bring cattle in, start a herd, how would he make sure the Indians didn't steal them, kill them the way they killed buffalo? Him and Shielle, they were a good team, but there were only two of them. Later, with any luck, they'd have kids, hopefully sons, who would be able to help him in time, but that was years and years ahead. If only little Joe . . .

A stabbing pain went through his heart as he thought of the son that he once did have and he shook his head and strode out with the horse in an effort to put the thought out of his mind. He was happy with Shielle and his new life, but sometimes, quite unexpectedly, the memory of his old life came back, memories of Mary, and little Joe, and then the wound hurt as much as ever — as if the event had happened only yesterday. Also, he realized, there was a feeling of guilt in his heart, as though he had betrayed Mary and little Joe by taking another woman, building another home, forgetting about them. He shook his head in perplexity as he tramped beside the horse's head. What was a man to do? How was he to live his life? How was he to deal with things when he didn't *know* what was the right thing to do?

"Whoah, now!" He hauled the horse up near the cabin. Better put useless thoughts out of his mind. He had work to do. Immediate work, that had to be done if he was to continue living. And that reminded him: he'd have to leave the place for a while, ride either to Fort Laramie or back east a-ways for powder and shot. He'd counted what he had left that morning. It was running mighty low. And their lives depended on it, for hunting. Yeah . . . and not only for hunting. For fighting. Because it was too much to hope that those Shoshone braves wouldn't come back. That wild bastard with the broken face . . . that was a vicious, vindictive character if he'd ever seen one. He'd be back. And he'd bring others with him. Wonder was they hadn't been back already . . .

He explained the situation to Shielle when they stopped for their midday meal. She had prepared rabbit stew, thickened with a little of their rapidly diminishing cornmeal, and wild onions. Communication was still far from easy because of the language difficulty but by making drawings in the earth and making signs they could make each other understand. And she was learning rapidly.

"Tomorrow. I go." He told her. "Powder and shot. For gun. Not much left. I go. Get powder and shot. Other things too." They did need a lot of things — pots and pans, knives, a spade for digging. And there were other things . . . things that they didn't actually need but that he'd like to get for her . . . a mirror — she'd like that — and maybe even some beads, a necklace. Crazy, maybe, but he knew she'd like that and he wanted to please her.

She nodded understanding and agreement then drew two figures in the dust. "Shielle go too," she said laboriously.

"No. Shielle go back to Sioux. Just for a little while. Then I come and take Shielle home. Here."

There was a row then, a little row made worse by her deep desire to be with him and by the difficulty in communication but eventually he prevailed over her and she agreed to go and stay with Deveraux and his woman until her man returned.

They rode out next morning, taking with them everything of value that they had. Bradley rode his own horse and led his pack horse while Shielle rode one pony and led the other. It took them two days to reach the Sioux village.

They were received with considerable interest. A small crowd gathered to watch them come in, someone ran to tell The Old Crow and she hobbled down to harangue them. Clearly the crowd were expecting some drama.

"Is all ri'," explained Deveraux with a grin. "They think you bring back woman because she is no good. Or because she no work. They watch for big row between you and The Old Crow."

"Then tell them they are wrong," said Bradley. "Tell them Shielle's the best woman in the whole Indian nation. I bring her here to be safe. She is too valuable to be left by herself while I am away. And Louis? Can she stay with you and your woman until I come back? I don't want The Old Crow to get the idea that Shielle is her slave again."

"Oui. She stay with us. I see she no work for Old Crow. But tonight, you and me, we eat with Many Wounds. Shielle stay in my lodge with my woman."

"If it's all the same to you, Louis,

I'd like fine to just stay with you too, overnight. Tell you the truth, I honestly ain't too happy here, in this village. I would take Shielle with me, only I can make better time on my own."

"Oui, I understan'!" Deveraux nodded sympathetically. "But is better we go eat with Many Wounds. He ask us, an' he no like if we don' go. Is big honour, to eat with him."

"He the chief or somethin'?"

Deveraux grinned. "He is one chief. Many chiefs here — The Lance Blade. The Bad Storm. Fighting Horse, and some others."

"Yeah? An' who's the *big* chief? I mean the boss."

"Hah!" Deveraux laughed openly. "Each one think he is boss."

"But which one do the braves follow?"

Deveraux shrugged. "Some follow Many Wounds, some follow The Bad Storm, some follow the others. Is same with Shoshone Indians. Some follow Bloody Hand, some follow other chiefs."

Bradley nodded. "Say," he asked gently, wishing to be as tactful as possible. "Is it . . . safe . . . here among these people? For white folks, I mean. I mean, they ain't likely to ever get hostile? Like them Shoshone Indians?"

Deveraux paused for a moment before he spoke, looking sober. "Indian is like white man," he explained. "Most of time he is happy to get along. He no like to get killed or hurt. But sometime if many Indian meet few white men . . . an' if white men have horses, mules, guns . . . then maybe Indian turn bad . . . Especially young braves. You know how it is with white men . . . especially young white men. Most white men, especially older men, no want trouble, no want fight. But young men some young men . . . no like that. They want fight. They no care 'bout hurt or die. Is true of white men, no?"

"Yeah." Bradley nodded grimly. "It's

true of white men. Guess it ain't reasonable to expect Indians to be any different."

That night he sat beside Many Wounds in the chief's crowded lodge. It was almost dark inside except for the dull red glow of the fire in the centre and the circulating red orb of the long pipe which Many Wounds had filled with *shongsasha* or red willow bark and which now passed from hand to hand as all the men smoked. Wooden bowls of boiled buffalo meat sat on the ground before them and Bradley was forced by politeness to dip his hands into the greasy mixture, carry some to his mouth and try to look appreciative.

From time to time an attentive squaw would drop some buffalo fat on to the dull embers of the fire and a bright yellow flame would leap up, illuminating for a few seconds the tall tepee with the chiefs weapons — bows, lances and axes — hung around the sides and the great conglomeration of curious Indians who had crowded into the tepee to observe the strange white-skin and to be present at the social occasion.

The entertainment went on well into the night with eating, smoking and old men chanting endlessly on in their guttural sing-song.

"They singing of big fights and great hunting, long time ago," Deveraux explained to him.

Bradley sat there in the gloom, nauseous with greasy meat, almost hypnotized by the never-ending chanting and his eyes smarting painfully from woodsmoke. His thoughts went to Shielle, and further back still to Mary and little Joe and his home at Saint Aubrey, Kansas. He looked at the lined, leathery-brown faces all around him in the smoky gloom and wondered what the hell he was doing here and how he came to be in this savage world.

In the morning he was up early, the Sioux village quiet all around him. He saddled his horses and, leaving the two ponies with Shielle, said his goodbyes to her. He got his directions from Deveraux at the edge of the village.

"For Fort Laramie, you ride north," explained the French-Canadian, throwing his head forward in that direction. "Always north. You know what is north?"

"Hell, yeah. I can tell north . . . I think. Most of the time anyways." Bradley looked around him. The morning was grey, chill and damp. Trees dripped forlornly; the Indian camp lay around him like a scattering of drab litter; further out the prospect was one of brown earth, trampled mud and long wet grass. He could summon up little enthusiasm for the journey ahead of him.

"Well, you ride always north," repeated Deveraux. "an' you follow the main trails. Okay? When you come to a trail that is bigger than the trail you are on, you take the bigger trail. Okay? And north." Again he gestured with the edge of his hand. "Always north. Maybe you meet someone from fort; then you ask; he tell you. If no, then you look. But you keep north, you keep to main trails — an' you fin' fort . . . in little time."

"How long do you reckon it'll take me?" Bradley felt like putting it off until Deveraux could accompany him. But it couldn't be put off, he knew that.

"To reach fort? To reach Laramee?" Deveraux put the accent on the syllable. "Ça depend. It depend. Maybe you find him quick; maybe you get lost a little. But . . . " he shrugged his shoulders, "maybe two-three day . . . maybe five-six day. But heh! What hell, eh?" he grinned. "One day, two day, no matter. She wait for you. We wait for you. Whole goddam village wait. World no go away, heh?"

"Yeah, I guess you're right, friend. An' now I guess I'd better get goin'. Sooner I leave the sooner I'm likely to get back." Bradley leaned down from his saddle and shook Deveraux warmly by the hand. "Take care of Shielle for me. An' thanks for everythin'."

"Is okay." The French-Canadian grinned, returning the handshake. "You take the great care. An' you come back real quick, oui?"

Bradley nodded without enthusiasm and kicked his horse into motion.

He rode all that day without stopping to eat, still slightly nauseous from the previous night's greasy meat, and towards nightfall huddled in his blanket beside a tiny fire and drank bitter black coffee. He had to let his horses graze but was constantly worried about possible Indian attack so he dozed only fitfully, rifle in hand, and moved position frequently to be near the browsing animals. He was in the saddle again at first light.

He rode north as instructed, using the sun and the moss on the tree trunks as his guide and sticking, as far as he could, to the trails.

They had originally been animal trails, he figured — made by buffalo, deer and wild horses — but these paths had been further trampled by Indians and maybe fur trappers — even a trading wagon or two.

Trouble was, they weren't there all the time: sometimes for miles they'd be clear as day, well-trodden paths marked by buffalo hoofs and horse-hoofs, maybe even showing a wagon track here and there; then, maybe because of ground that was too hard, or ground that was too soft — or for no goddam reason at all as far as he could see — they just wouldn't be there any more, and he'd have to go back and try to pick up where he'd left off. And sometimes he'd get downright lost and wouldn't know where in hell he was in that wilderness, so he'd just look round till he found a trail and follow that as long as it went north. But this meant a lot of back-tracking and riding across country and after three days' riding he had to admit that he had little idea of how far he'd come or how far he still had to go.

Jesus! The world was a goddam big place. He hadn't realized that, back in Kansas. An' it all looked the goddam same — long stretches of grassy prairie, gentle hills clothed in timber, shallow gullies holding little creeks fringed with cottonwoods — so you couldn't tell if you were ridin' round in goddam circles! But he rode on, day after day, through the endlessly similar countryside, apparently getting nowhere, and then one day he rode down a trail like a hundred others, round a bend like a thousand more, and came across a little clutter of wagons huddling in the shelter of a damp, muddy hill.

He checked his mount in surprise. He couldn't believe it! A minute ago there had been nothing. Only himself in this wilderness. Now, all of a sudden, as if they had been dropped from the sky, here were wagons, horses, people.

At least he supposed there were people — must be people, he told himself, though at first glance he couldn't see any.

Funny, too, now that the first shock of realization was over, the wagons looked — derelict. They were drawn off the trail a few yards and untidily arranged, as though the people who had positioned them had had other things on their mind at the time.

They had been there for some time too, by the look of them. A couple had tarpaulins stretched over the ends to give them additional protection. One had a sorry-looking lean-to extension built on to the end with green branches. A small, ramshackle corral had been scraped together with assorted brushwood and inside it stood several wretched horses and mules, hanging their heads in silent misery. The place had the look — and the smell — of defeat and abandonment.

Bradley edged his mount nearer. "Hello the camp!" he called. There was no answer but he caught sight of a flutter of movement behind one of the tarpaulins. "Hello the camp!" he called again, reining in and sitting still in the saddle. "I'm just by myself," he added, knowing how he himself would feel at the sight of strangers. "Just one man. Joe Bradley. Trying to get to Fort Laramie . . . an' kinda lost. Ain't meanin' no harm to nobody. You got my word."

There was a grunting, muttering sound from close by . . . a human voice, but saying things he couldn't make out. Still no human beings appeared.

"Is there somebody there . . . anybody aroun'? You don' min' if I get down?" Bradley called out plainly to the empty air, turning his head in a half-circle to scan the several wagons — five of them altogether, he counted, in two groups, three in one, two in another. There was a groaning and a hoarse muttering, the sound of slow, painful movement. It seemed to come from the nearest of the group of two wagons. Bradley dismounted stiffly and moved cautiously towards the sound and a girl came into view from behind one of the tarpaulins among the other group of wagons. She had a rifle pointed at him.

"Wh . . . What do you want? Who are you? What . . . want?" Her voice was hoarse and frightened and died away altogether in places.

Bradley stood still where he was, conscious of the trembling rifle in unreliable hands. That gun could go off and he was in the way.

"My name's Joe Bradley, Ma'am," he answered, clear and calm. "Like I said, I'm tryin' to git to Fort Laramie but I'm kinda lost. I'm new to these parts. Come from Kansas. A farmer. Jus' happened to stumble in here. You got trouble?" He turned his head slowly to indicate the wretched animals in the corral. "Stock ain't in good shape." The farmer in him abhorred the idea of livestock being neglected. "Think maybe I could help."

"Don't try nothin' fresh!" The drooping rifle muzzle was brought up again with a jerk. "We've got menfolks here, several of them, right here . . . an' they can all shoot . . . " The girl started suddenly to cry and the rifle muzzle dropped till it was pointing halfway to the ground. Loud, ugly weeping sounds came from her and she just stood there, her head sinking on to her breast and her shoulders shaking.

"Hey, it's all right, Ma'am." Bradley responded spontaneously, his concern genuine and unselfish. "You don't have to worry 'bout me. I ain't gonna hurt nobody. Try to help, if I can. What's wrong? You in trouble?"

There was a grunt and a scuffle and a dirty, hairy paw of a hand appeared over the edge of the tailboard of the nearest wagon. Some anguished grunting then a soft thud of collapse, as though someone had fallen.

Bradley moved cautiously forward and parted the canvas flaps and looked inside. A bad smell engulfed him. The inside of the wagon was a disorderly mess. Lying prostrate on the floor, his hand stretched out towards the light, was a half-dressed man. He was skeletally thin, his face black with bristle and dirt, his eyes huge in sunken sockets. His mouth gaped in anguish, his few teeth showing yellow and black. "Water!" the word was a breathless sigh. "Water . . . for the love of God. Water."

8

SHIELLE and the girl known as White-Robe sat by the side of the stream and chattered endlessly, the jars they had brought to fill with water forgotten on the bank. White-Robe was full of questions. Was the lodge of the whiteskin, Shielle's man, a good lodge? How big was it? Did it keep the rain out? And did Shielle have many pots — of the kind that the whiteskins had, made of that strange, marvellous material that never cracked? Was Shielle's man a good provider? Surely with those guns he would shoot many buffalo? And was he a good man, a kind man? Did he beat her often?

Shielle was as eager to answer as White-Robe was to ask. Yes, they had a fine lodge, and it stayed in the same place all the time: they were not going to move it, never. And they only had one wonderful pot at present but Joe — that was her mans name, Joe — had gone to the big whiteskin village far away to get many things. He would bring back many pots, and knives, and blankets — Oh! And lots of other things. He hadn't actually said anything, but — and here Shielle hung her head a little and looked decidedly shy — something in the way he had spoken and behaved had caused her to think that he might bring back something specially for her . . . some clothes such as the whiteskin women wore maybe, or some beads.

White-Robe was keenly interested. Shielle, she said, was very lucky. White-Robe herself would like to have such a man. And how did they live? What did Shielle cook for him? And did Shielle grow maize and beans? And was there no danger in living away from the village? No. There wouldn't be any danger: the whiteskin was a great warrior, everyone knew of how he had fought many of the hated Shoshone.

No, they didn't have a maize or bean patch yet, Shielle admitted, but when her man returned and took her home, then they would start one. And it was true that there was no danger: no one had troubled them during the time they had stayed there together. Everyone knew that her man, Joe, was a great warrior.

It was at that point that the idea came to Shielle. Why didn't she go back to her new home — and take White-Robe with her? Then White-Robe could see the new lodge for herself. It was perfectly safe, and they had the two ponies. They needn't stay long, just a day or two.

White-Robe gasped at the thought. Yes! And they could start a maize and bean patch! The two of them together! Then it would be ready for Shielle's man when he got back from the big whiteskin village with all the pots and knives and blankets . . . and beads. The idea of beads particularly appealed to White-Robe. If beads were being given out then might not a girl who had helped to make a maize and bean patch expect some reward?

Shielle's enthusiasm flamed. Yes! Why not? And White-Robe could stay with Shielle in her new lodge and sleep beside her in that wonderful bed! Oh! They would have a lovely time. And they had the two ponies.

White-Robe's lips compressed thoughtfully. Ah, but there was a difficulty. Maybe the other whiteskin, the one they called Deveraux, maybe he would not let them go?

Yes . . . that was true, Shielle admitted. Joe, her man, had told her to stay with Deveraux and his woman, Clever Hands. But Deveraux was going out with his gun tomorrow, he would be away for a long time. They could slip away after Deveraux had left the village. And they would only stay away for one or two days, then they would come back again and everything would be all right. Why shouldn't they do it? It would be fun, and it would be safe, and everything would be all right!

White-Robe nodded excitedly, proud to be sought out as a friend to the woman of the great warrior and enviously anxious to see the fine lodge and the wonderful bed. Besides, there was the possibility of those beads . . . Yes! Why didn't they slip away quietly, after Deveraux had gone out with his gun?

No reason at all, said Shielle. And they began to make their plans.

* * *

Bradley threw the final shovelfuls of dirt on to the mound and slammed the earth firm with the back of the spade. 'Pity there weren't no rocks handy,' he thought. 'Might have kept the wolves and coyotes away.' On the other hand, it looked as if these people — and himself — were going to be here for some time, so maybe the wolves would lose interest. He laid the spade down and picked up the plain wooden cross that he had made the night before. Painted on it in tar were the words: *Lizy Gaston, aged 26, from Dayton, Ohio. Died here on way to Oregon. Sept. 1844*.

Bradley studied it for a moment then walked slowly over to the group of three wagons. "Ma'am?" he called. "Miss Maxwell? You there?"

The tarpaulin stretched over the end of the wagon was pushed aside and the girl appeared, gaunt, drawn, her black hair pulled tightly back from her pale face. "Yes?"

Bradley indicated the wooden cross. "That look all right to you, Ma'am? I ain't one for the readin' an' writin'."

She looked at it and nodded. "It's fine." There was a pause then she said with a rush: "It's good of you to do the buryin'. I couldn't. I didn't have the strength. It was all I could do to drag her out of the wagon. I wasn't sure that that was the best thing . . . I mean with wolves an' all that . . . but I couldn't leave her there . . . not with me workin' aroun' the place . . . " She shuddered and almost broke down then took a grip on herself again.

"You did jus' fine, Ma'am." Bradley looked around the clearing at the three grave mounds. "Who were the other two?"

"One is Mother's. Mr Harris and Dad buried her. Then Mr Harris got sick himself. Dad and Mr Clare buried him. Now they're sick too . . . an' Mrs Clare an' Mrs Harris. I'm the only one that hasn't got it."

"How did it happen, Ma'am? I mean, well . . . " It was a crazy question. How did disease happen? Did it matter how it happened?

"We were part of a bigger wagon train, going to Oregon, or California . . . some hadn't quite made up their minds. And the sickness just broke out . . . just the Clares' wagon at first, then the Gastons', then these others. They put us to the back of the train, to avoid further infection. But we couldn't keep up . . . just kept falling further and further behind. Then we got lost. Don't ask me how we got lost, I don't know. But we did. And we straggled along by ourselves for . . . oh, a few days, I suppose. Then Mother died. We stopped here to bury her . . . an' the sickness spread. We weren't fit to go on. So we just stayed here, because there was water. Then Mr Harris died, an' now . . . "

She broke off and looked towards the latest grave.

Bradley studied the pale, drawn face. "You eatin' Ma'am? An' drinkin', an' sleepin'? You got to, you know . . . if you're gonna go on workin' way you are." A thought struck him. "It wouldn't be the water, Ma'am? I mean it wouldn't be bad water, would it?"

"I don't think so. The sickness broke out before we got here, and we've been using that little creek all the time we've been here. But I don't know, I don't know nothin' 'bout med'cine. Do you?" She looked at him without much hope.

Bradley shook his head. "No, Ma'am. I guess I don't. But I know that people got to eat an' drink an' sleep, if they're gonna keep goin'. You see that you do. I'd invite you to eat with me but I reckon it's better to keep the two groups of wagons apart, way they are now. Less risk of infection that way. You look after your folks an' I'll look after the other two. How are your people today, anyway?"

"Dad's just the same . . . got it kinda bad, but he's holdin' his own. Mrs Harris seems to be a little better, but it's hard to say. Mr an' Mrs Clare don't seem to be no worse . . . they been like that for days now. Maybe they'll start to get better soon. How are your people?"

"Well, they ain't in good shape, that's a fact. That man, one I gave the water to . . . What didja say his name was?"

"Mr Embers. Harry Embers."

"Yeah, him. He's in a poor way. Other man . . . Mr Gaston? . . . he ain't as bad but he ain't good neethur. It could go eethur way with both of 'em." Bradley studied the girl again. "You been runnin' this show all on your own, past few days?"

"I've been the only one fit to get up and move about. I wouldn't say I've been runnin' things: just doin' what I could . . . boiling the water . . . tryin' to get them to drink . . . take a little soup . . . sleep. What else could I do?"

"You been doin' all right." She was a quality woman, Bradley decided. He was a man who always recognised quality, whether in animals or humans — it was the farmer in him, he supposed. Many another woman would have broken down in these circumstances but she had done what she could. Had been a good lookin' woman, too, before she'd got sick herself. He noted the erect carriage, the high bosom and generous hips. He reprimanded himself silently and sharply: he had a woman already . . . an' that reminded him: he oughta be gettin' back to her . . . hadn't intended to be away this long. But he couldn' go just yet, couldn' leave these people like this.

He smiled at the girl. "Well, you see you get enough to eat, an' get what sleep you can. Maybe some wagons'll come by this way. They're comin' all the time now. That way we could get more help. Meantime, we'll both do what we can." He turned and went to put up the simple cross.

Later, back in Harry Embers' wagon, he tried to get the gaunt, emaciated man to swallow some cornmeal mush but his patient nearly choked, letting the gruel spill out of his mouth and run down his shirt front. All he wanted to do was drink.

"Yeah . . . you gotta drink all right," Bradley muttered to himself, "but you gotta have nourishment too, if you're gonna live. Wish I could get some fresh meat. Maybe make some thin stew. That might help." The migrants had a fair supply of flour, dried meat and cornmeal but no fresh meat.

Over the next few days he took his rifle and went out looking for game but had no luck, so he had to resort to steeping dried salt beef in water for days then making a thin stew with wild onions and a little flour added. He managed to get Harry Embers and the man in the other wagon, Frank Gaston, to swallow a little but it did not seem to do much for their general condition.

He also tidied up Embers' wagon. It needed it, having the look of a house that had never known order. There hadn't been any Mrs Embers, he guessed, not with a wagon like that. Everything was thrown together in hopeless confusion, firearms jostling for space with bolts of cloth, horse harness competing for space with fishing nets and a sewing machine, farming tools lying side by side with a ramshackle, home-made whisky still — and all of it ill-kept, neglected and dirty. What kind of a man was this, Bradley wondered, and what was he going to Oregon to *do*?

Not that there wasn't some good stuff in the wagon. Bradley's eyes, long used to want and insufficiency, lit up at the sight of some of the items — several excellent pots and pans including a fine skillet; a pair of field glasses that must have been army property at one time; a magnificent cross-cut saw and two smaller hand-saws; fishing poles and hooks and line; coils of new rope; two small barrels of powder and two sacks of shot; a cavalry sabre in its scabbard with the belt attached; horse-shoeing materials; a grindstone for sharpening axes and scythes. Bradley felt a gentle touch of envy. What a godsend those things would be to someone like himself. He only hoped that Embers would make good use of them in Oregon. If he ever got there.

That wasn't certain, he decided. The man had lost a great deal of weight and he was eating virtually nothing. He had become a wasted scarecrow, possessed by a raging thirst. He couldn't go on like this . . . he was a tough bird all right, otherwise he wouldn't have lasted as long as this — but it couldn't go on . . .

Bradley tried talking to him in an effort to encourage him and, strangely enough, the man seemed very willing to talk, as far as his weakened condition would allow.

"You . . . goin' . . . Or'gon?" he croaked out to Bradley one afternoon as Bradley supported his head and tried to ease some thin stew-gravy down the tortured throat. "You got . . . wagon . . . people?"

"Naw." Bradley shook his head. "I jus' happened along. Was ridin' to Fort Laramie, an' got lost."

"You stay." The words were only just audible. "Stay. I get better. Give you money. You stay, eh?"

"Aw, I'll stay a while. Don' want no money though. Money ain't no good to me. Ain't no stores where I live.

But don' you worry now. Jus' take it easy an' get well. I'll be here for a while yet."

The sick man clutched his arm feverishly. "You stay. I give you money . . . when I get . . . better. You want . . . gun? I give . . . you . . . gun. An' powder . . . an' . . . shot too . . . all kinda things . . . if you . . . stay."

"Take it easy, Mr Embers," Bradley cautioned him. "Don' be givin' all your stuff away. You're gonna need it all when you get to Oregon. You a farmer? Horse rancher?"

The sick man gave him a strange, almost suspicious look. Naw . . . I'm . . . I'm . . . Nothin'." He turned his head deliberately away from Bradley.

"Aw, you're feelin' bad right now," Bradley consoled him, "but it ain't gonna last for ever. You'll be back to bein' your ol' self in a few days, you'll see. Jus' rest now." He lowered the heavy head to the pillow and drew the blanket up to the bristly chin. The wide, frightened eyes closed in something like sleep.

He sure was a strange one, Bradley thought as he went towards the other wagon. He had a gunshot wound in his chest, few years old. Maybe he'd been in the army at one time. And there were cuts on his arms that could have been knife cuts and a bad scar on his scalp. He'd seen action all right, Bradley reflected. He himself knew enough about it to recognize the signs, he thought ruefully.

His other patient, Frank Gaston, was a little better, though dangerously exhausted. He took a little nourishment and was able to talk to him, though very weakly. He was a blacksmith-farrier, going to set up in Oregon or California. At least that had been his intention, but now, having lost his wife, he wasn't so sure. Maybe he'd go back to Illinois . . . if he lived.

"Aw, you'll live," Bradley assured him. "I figger you're over the worst of it. You'll see, you'll feel a little better every day from now on."

"Good job you came along, son." He was only a few years older than Bradley. "I reckon we'd a been done for."

"Aw, I din't do much. Only fetched water, done a little bit cookin' . . . " He could have added that he'd buried the dead, seen to the livestock, tidied up the mess and risked infection in order to feed them, but he did not even think of this.

"You did more'n that, son. You brought us hope, encouragement. You don' know how important that is. But wasn't you scared? I mean of catchin' it. Whatever it is?"

"Well . . . I guess I didn' think of that. I s'pose that if these things are gonna get you they're gonna get you," he added lamely. It was true that he hadn't thought of the risk of infection. And when he *did* think of it he figgered it was too late: either he had caught the disease or he hadn't. Either way it didn't matter. And he couldn't just ride on his way and leave these people to die. Maybe the presence of a good-looking woman had something to do with it, he thought uncomfortably.

"Well, got no more time for jawin' right now," he told his patient. "I got horses an' mules to see to."

He climbed down from the wagon and went towards the corral, feeling strangely cheerful. It was good to be amongst his own kind of people.

* * *

They sat around in an untidy jumble, touching up their warpaint and waiting for the return of the scout, their ponies tearing at the grass nearby. Bloody Hand went to and fro amongst them, nodding in approval at the painted faces, encouraging them, reassuring them with a firm grasp of hand on arm. Yes, it was almost time; after two days' riding they were near the place, were only waiting for the scout's report. They were brave warriors, he told them. Not like some other Shoshones, who were like old women. And they would reap their reward. The whiteskin had many guns and many horses and when they had killed him they would share these things amongst them. Not that they had to fear the guns, he assured them, seeing apprehension behind the paint on some faces, because, as they all knew, a gun could only fire once, then some time had to pass before it could be fired again. And they were many, and the whiteskin was only one. Here he saw the apprehension fade and be replaced by bravado. Aaaaiiiieeee! Bloody Hand exclaimed, it was said that this whiteskin was a great warrior, but what would the Shoshone maids think when these braves returned home with his horses and guns — and his scalp! Some yelling followed this comment and the braves drummed on the ground with the butts of their lances. Some even jumped to their feet and did a spontaneous dance. Bloody Hand nodded approval, his broken face grotesque in paint: they were working up nicely.

In the middle of their preparation the scout returned. Yes, the whiteskin was there — must be there, because there were two squaws there, doing women's work, digging and planting. No, he hadn't actually seen the whiteskin; he must be in his lodge. But he would be there, must be there if the squaws were there . . .

Bloody Hand nodded. He couldn't call off the raid now . . . now that they were all worked up. And the whiteskin would be there . . . in his lodge . . . Well, so much the better. He shouted the order and pointed to the ponies. There were yells and screams and the twenty braves ran eagerly to mount.

He had some difficulty holding them in but managed to keep them in hand until they got to the place. There he spaced them out, surrounding the clearing, their weapons ready. The ponies were prancing, the warriors panting, grunting, striking imaginary blows. He couldn't hold them much longer, in a few minutes more they would spontaneously explode. He looked around the clearing but saw no sign of his hated enemy. The ponies were jumping and wheeling their riders gasping and striking . . . They would lose control in a . . .

"Aaaiiieeeeh!" he screamed, driving his heels into his frantic pony and bounding ahead, whirling his axe in the air. There was a crashing and pounding, a demented chorus of yells and screams and the charge was under way.

* * *

Bradley unloaded the raw, bloody load from his pack-horse. He'd been lucky to get a buffalo, even a bull, although he had hoped for a cow: the cow meat was richer, fatter, more succulent. Still, they now had fresh meat. Maybe it wasn't too late, even yet, for Harry Embers.

He left a load for the girl, outside her wagon, and put some on to cook. He hung the rest on lines strung between the wagons, to dry.

When the stew was ready he poured some of the gravy into a tin cup and went into Embers' wagon. His heart sank when he saw the condition of the man. Jesus! He couldn't last much longer at this rate.

Again he tried to feed him, holding his head in the crook of his arm and trying to direct a little of the gravy down the contracted throat. Embers turned his head away in pain and hopelessness but Bradley persisted and managed, perhaps, to get a little of the liquid into the empty stomach. Then, feeling it was useless to continue further, he laid the man down again and went into the other wagon to see Frank Gaston. Gaston was a little better and able to sit up and feed himself with a little of the stew. Bradley chatted to him for a few minutes to cheer him up, then went back to the Embers' wagon.

As soon as he entered he knew that Embers' condition had suddenly deteriorated and when he sat down beside the sick man he knew that death was imminent. Embers looked at him with brightened eyes; his voice, when he spoke, was stronger, but Bradley knew, intuitively, that it was not the strength of recovery, but the false improvement that sometimes comes just before death. He gave up, for the moment, any idea of feeding the sick man and automatically began to fulfil the role of comforter.

"Well, Harry," he began, "you're talkin' a mite better today, huh? What's on your mind?"

The skinny, knife-scarred arm reached out. The skeletal hand closed weakly on Bradley's arm. "Wan' you to stay . . . Little while . . . Won't be long now . . . You'll stay?"

"Sure." Bradley smiled and gripped

the bony shoulder in a gesture of warm friendship. "I jus' got a coupla little chores to do an' then I'll come an . . .

"Naw!" The word came out strong, anxious. "Don't go. Don' go now. Stay. I'm a goin' . . . dyin' . . . know it. Don' wan' to die alone. Stay, Mister . . . Please . . . I'm a-beggin' ya."

"Aw, hell! You ain't dyin'." Bradley tried to sound convincing. "But okay! I'll stick aroun' a while. Chores can wait. Time I set down a while."

"You . . . You ain't a preacher?" The sick man's eyes were bright with anxiety. "Are ya? Ever been a preacher?"

Bradley shook his head ruefully. "Naw," he admitted. "I ain't never been any kind of church man."

"I'd a liked a preacher," sighed Embers. "Got things to tell him." He looked cautiously at Bradley. "I ain't lived a good life."

"Well . . . " Bradley gently pushed the damp hair out of the dying man's eyes. "We ain't none of us angels. I guess we all goin' to be in need of a little forgiveness. But folks — preachers even — tell me we got that comin'. I guess we'll be all right."

"Stay with me," said the dying man. "When I'm gone . . . you can have the wagon . . . team . . . all this stuff . . . "

"Ain't you got no kin?" Bradley asked gently.

"Naw. Nobody who'd want to know me." He looked away and looked back again quickly. "I killed a man in Saint Louis." His eyes watched Bradley fearfully for his reaction.

The shock faded quickly for Bradley. "Well . . . I killed coupla men myself," he murmured thoughtfully. "Indians."

"I'm a-talkin' 'bout a white man . . . decent white man. I killed two more in Abilene, an' wounded a few here an' there. I've lived a bad life . . . been a bad, bad man."

Bradley felt increasingly uncomfortable. This was more than he had bargained for.

"Worst of all was Kansas," sighed the dying man. "Place called Saint Aubrey." His voice almost died away.

"You say Saint Aubrey?" Bradley's own voice was a gasp.

"Yeah. Jus' outside. Me an' Burden . . . an' Bandy . . . an' Kowalski . . . I wish to Jesus we hadn' . . . but we did. Me too, I was as bad as the rest . . . "

Bradley could hardly get the words out. "Was it a farm? Little farm? Jus' a woman . . . an' a kid? No men aroun'?"

"Yeah . . . yeah. You sure you ain't a preacher? I wish to Jesus there was a preacher. But I'll tell you — you can tell the preacher for me, huh? You'll stay, huh? Can take the wagon an' the stuff when I'm gone." The voice died away again.

"What about Saint Aubrey?" There was a hard edge to Bradley's voice, an edge that he could not keep out, however hard he tried.

"I quit then. That's when I quit."

The voice was uneven, now fading, now recovering, and hoarse all the time. "Couldn' stand it no more. Hadda quit. Went back east, bought this wagon an' stuff. Was gonna make a new start in Cal'forny . . . but I guess it was no good. You can't . . . rub out . . . an' ol', bad life. I didn' kill nobody there, though, that's a fact. It was Bandy shot the kid . . . an' Kowalski killed the woman. I quit after that . . . went back east . . . They went on west . . . "

"Who went on west? Tell me!" Bradley had to control himself. He was shaking the dying man.

The man's breath was going, his voice fading. "Burden, Pike Burden. Pike was the boss. He picked all the places, took the lead. We followed him . . . wasn' unwillin' neethur."

"Who else was with you, with Pike Burden? At Saint Aubrey?"

"Eh . . . Kowalski . . . killed the woman . . . but it was Bandy who killed the kid. That's what made me quit . . . couldn't go on after that . . . went back east . . . was gonna . . . ”

“Where were they headed — Burden and Kowalski an’ . . . ”

The dying man shook his head weakly. “Don’ rightly know. They was gonna hole up a while at a li’l place near Laramie . . . Peek’s Place . . . somethin’ like that. Say, you ain’t a preacher are you . . . Naw . . . you said . . . But stay, Mister, don’ let me die alone. I ain’t been a good man . . . but I quit after that . . . couldn’ go on. You can have this wagon . . . all this stuff . . . ”

“Peek’s Place? That what it’s called? Near Fort Laramie?” He was afraid the man would die before he found out.

“Yeah . . . somethin’ like that. Say, Mister . . . you know any prayers? You say somethin’ for me, huh? I’m a-goin’ . . . know it . . . Say somethin’ . . . you can have this wagon an’ stuff . . . I wish to Jesus I hadn’t done them things. You think Jesus’ll believe me? Say a prayer, Mister . . . Please!”

Bradley lowered his head and began

to mumble the only religious words he knew: "The Lord is my Shepherd, I'll not want . . . " and behind him he could hear the hoarse utterances: " . . . my Shepherd . . . not want . . . " His face was contorted and ugly with tears and grief but whether the grief was for his dead wife and son or the dying man beside him . . . or for both of them — nobody could have said.

* * *

Later, after the burial, he stood outside the Maxwells' wagon and explained to the girl. "I got to go, Ma'am. Been away too long. An' I got things to do, back home. Mr Gaston, he's doin' all right, be okay. An' your paw . . . an' the Clares. Probably be a wagon train along in a little while. But I got to go, really."

"You takin' the wagon he left you?"

"Naw. I'm in too much a hurry. Got a bad feelin'."

"But you'll come back — I mean to

see if we're all right?"

"Well, I'll try, Ma'am, I'll . . . "

"Mary." She smiled for the first time. "My name's Mary."

"Well, Mary. I'll try. Lots of things can happen, as you know. But I'll try to get back . . . see that you get outa here . . . an' get my wagon . . . I'll try Ma'am."

9

HE began looking for tell-tale signs as soon as he began to recognise the landmarks and knew that he was nearing home. At first he didn't know that he was doing it, but after a while he couldn't deny to himself that his frequent glances skywards were intended to spot any buzzard activity.

"I'm crazy," he told himself. "Been among sick people too long. Git to imagining that things is wrong somewhere. I'll be awright when I get among ordinary folks again." But as he rode on, recognising increasingly the familiar landmarks, his heart beat a bit faster and he felt distinctly jumpy.

There were no buzzards to be seen. That was reassuring. Still he wasn't comfortable. He'd stayed away too long, far too goddam long. But what else could he have done? He argued with himself constantly as he urged his mount forward, Jesus! Would he never get there?

At first sight the place looked unchanged and he felt a little easing of the tension. It looked slightly different from what he remembered, but then he'd been away some time, and the grass had grown and in a way he was seeing it with different eyes.

He had to ride almost to the door of the cabin before he became aware of the signs of violation. The logs, too green to burn, were here and there blackened and scorched by fire, the door that had been new when he left leaned to one side, one leather hinge broken.

He swept the area with an uncertain glance. The corral rails were knocked down in places . . . someone had been here . . . someone had been wreaking destruction. His heart sank.

Still, if this was all the damage . . . His spirits rose slightly: maybe it wasn't surprising: after all, in a land like this, if a man left his property for two-three weeks . . . well, wasn't surprising that a few marauding Indians . . . But he'd been wise to leave Shielle with Deveraux and the Sioux.

He dismounted and went into the cabin and rage blossomed within him. The place had been despoiled. The bed-framework had been smashed and the pieces strewn on the floor; the buffalo-hide window covers had been torn down and ripped to pieces; one wall had been shoved apart from the others so that a great gap of daylight showed; people had defecated over the floor in several places and stamped plainly on the walls and on the inside of the door was the shape of a hand, in bright red ochre.

He stood silent for a moment taking in the obscenity, then he began to swear. He swore fiercely and vehemently, clenching his fists and mentally murdering the offenders then he turned and ran out of the place. He ran to the corral and looked about him, not sure of what he was looking for. Nothing to see there . . . grass trampled into mud . . . rails pulled down . . . he knew that already.

Then he saw the buzzards. No wonder he hadn't seen them in the sky: they were all on the ground, forty yards from the cabin, among some scant brush, busy about their work.

Even then he didn't know. After all, there had been no one there. Who . . . ? What . . . ? It didn't make sense.

He could only tell that the two bodies had been women . . . could tell that by the clothes. The buzzards and other scavengers had been too busy for any other identification to be possible.

Deveraux would know! Deveraux would be able to reassure him! He must go to the Sioux village at once. Deveraux would clear up this terrible confusion. But first he'd have to bury these violated bodies: it was just possible — just *possible* — it wasn't a *fact* — because Shielle had been with Deveraux, at the Sioux village! It couldn't possibly . . .

With hope and disbelief struggling in his heart with fear and despair he ran to his horses and, clambering into the saddle, spurred urgently away from the contaminated place.

With tired horses it took him more than forty-eight hours to reach the Sioux village and by that time he knew the truth in his heart: he just needed to have it confirmed.

Deveraux's first glance confirmed it. The Canadian greeted him with a marked apprehension. "Shielle is with you, no?" The hesitant smile could not hide the gravity on the face behind it.

"Naw. She's with you." Maybe if he insisted on it it would be true. "I left her here, with you, an' your woman. She's still here. Must be."

But she wasn't.

He didn't need any further explanation.

He knew now. He hardly heard Deveraux's excuses, of how he had gone out with his gun, of how he had met up with two trappers, of how they had gone off together looking for buffalo, of how they had eventually ended up at Fort Laramie, expecting to see Bradley there, of how they had got drunk and stayed for several days . . . He didn't even remember leaving the place. It was like the first time, when he'd lost his wife and child, all over again; he was sort of blacked out, as if in a living dream. A man can only stand so much; beyond a certain point something takes over to prevent his total destruction.

When he came to his senses he was sitting with his back against a tree, his two horses grazing nearby. He rose and unsaddled then made camp. There were lots of supplies on the pack horse and he lit a small fire and cooked food and spread his blanket in a comfortable place. He did everything carefully and deliberately: he knew what he had to do now, and knew that he would have to be fed and rested to carry it out properly.

* * *

It took him four days to locate the Shoshone village, four days of patient riding and scouting. When he had found it he lay in deep cover and observed it through the field-glasses he had inherited from Harry Embers. It was just another Indian village, as far as he could see, except for the fact that there seemed to be a party of braves in it who regularly assembled together. They seemed to be held in high esteem by the other Indians. He studied them carefully for several days but couldn't determine much about them. But he waited, cold and patient, working his way nearer to observe more closely. He slept at night, ate jerky and drank only cold water. He had to be rested, had to be fed, had to be fit for the challenge that lay ahead of him. So he saw to his horses, saw to his own needs, and waited.

The proof came to him in time. One day the braves mounted and he saw on the rump of the leader's pony the bloody red hand. He nodded grimly, knowing the time had come.

He watched the direction they took from the village, then went to his horses. He tightened the cinches on his saddle horse, took the cavalry sabre that had lately been the property of Harry Embers and girded it on. He checked his rifle and pistols — his own and one he had got from Embers — saw that they were loaded and primed then mounted and rode out.

He wouldn't have too far to ride, because they were coming in his direction — probably going back to his homestead, looking to see if he was there this time; they'd be bucked up by their earlier success and keen to try to repeat it. "Well, come on," he muttered to himself as he rode on. "Come and get me. I ain't gonna be hard to find."

He stopped on the wide prairie where it was dotted by thick clumps of trees and took cover in a wood close to and facing down the trail. 'Horse gonna call out when he sees and smells their ponies,' he thought to himself. 'But I gotta chance that. Can't do nothin' about it.' He checked his rifle and pistols again: all loaded and primed. He dismounted and, taking a sack from his packhorse, grained the two horses. He patted their necks as they ground their oats. They'd been two good horses. Pity he was going to part company with them but it looked as if he had finally come to the end of the line.

He reloaded the sack on the pack-saddle and considered tethering the pack-horse to a tree but decided against it: he probably wouldn't be around to untie him when this job was done and he didn't want the animal to suffer distress. He checked that the sabre at his belt could be drawn freely and then squatted down to wait.

About ten minutes later he heard the bony clatter of the unshod hoofs. They were coming. This was it. He climbed into the saddle and sat with his rifle across the pommel, the two pistols stuck in his belt.

They came on, unsuspecting, about twenty of them. Soon he could see their weirdly painted faces. The broken-faced one, Bloody Hand, was in the front rank, flanked by two or three henchmen. Their ponies, small, lean and spirited, shook their heads and half-pranced in their freshness; feathers and fur decked their manes and tails. They clattered up the trail towards him, eager and unaware.

He waited till they were only forty yards away, amazed that his horse had not called out. He'd already gained the advantage of surprise.

He raised the rifle and levelled it, sighting right in the middle of Bloody Hand's body. "Come on," he murmured, holding the weapon rock steady. "Just a little bit more, to be sure, then come and receive your death." He held the weapon in place a fraction of a second longer then squeezed the trigger. He heard the roar of the shot and saw Bloody Hand jerk suddenly and topple to the side, then he threw the rifle down on the ground, drew one pistol with his left hand and the sabre with his right and spurred his mount straight at his enemies.

They had reined in in consternation, shock and surprise registering on their faces in spite of the fierce warpaint there. For a few seconds they darted glances from one to the other, their ponies milling in confusion, then they broke and scattered. Most of them were riding away from him, riding hell-for-leather and shit-scared, his reputation and sudden appearance demoralizing them completely. Others, given no time to choose, found themselves facing him and forced to fight. But, like himself in similar circumstances, when they were in they were in.

Bradley saw a black-and-red face

above a white-striped torso and fired his pistol point-blank into the body. The next instant he swung the sabre in a savage cut and saw it cleave a brave half-through the neck. Blows were raining on him, things sticking into him, so that for a second he thought he was falling from his horse. He recovered, and bringing the point of the sabre up drove it deep into a vermilion-streaked midriff. The blade stuck and as he wrestled to free it he saw a wolfskin-covered head rise over him and felt a terrible blow on his shoulder. He grabbed his other pistol with his free hand and shot the wolfskin-covered brave close up, in the belly. The stink of burning flesh in his nostrils, he heaved his sabre free and wheeled his horse round. There was a turmoil of bodies and struggling ponies on the ground. Half-trapped amongst this living debris several braves were struggling in confusion, unable to attack or retreat. Bradley spurred straight at them, riding over the bodies on the ground and lusting for destruction. Two braves broke free and tried to flee. He caught up with them and heaved one off his pony with his shoulder, cutting him deep on the arm as he passed. Sabre levelled, he charged the other's retreating back and drove the bloody blade deep into the unresisting flesh just above the breech-clout.

He checked his horse and wheeled it savagely round again. The only braves in sight were fleeing, riding terrified away from him. Without a second's thought he spurred his shuddering nervous horse after them, seeking death, his own or theirs. By savage rowelling of his mount he caught up with the stragglers. The brave just in front of him cast a terrified glance behind him, causing his pony to stumble and falter. Bradley swung the sabre with all his strength and saw it cleave deep into the brave's ribs, under his arm. The Indian fell screaming from his pony. Bradley checked his mount and wheeled. A brave, trying to flee but confused by fear, was charging straight at him. Bradley levelled the sabre and spurred to meet the charge. The brave threw up his hands, screaming, but, unable to stop, impaled himself on the sabre and fell howling from the saddle, pulling the sabre from Bradley's grasp.

He leapt from the saddle and hauled the blade from the warm body of the screaming Indian, then, heaving himself back into the saddle, looked round for other targets but found that there were none: the field was his, once again.

Still his vengeance was not satisfied. He spurred his spent horse in the direction of the fleeing warriors but could not come up with any. To and fro he rode, seeking any encounter he might find but finding none. Back he rode, slowly now, to the scene of the struggle and finding wounded braves attempting to crawl away cut them down finally and determinedly with his bloody blade.

Searching the gory carnage for his arch-enemy he found Bloody Hand lying face down, painted face contorted with agony and his life-blood staining the earth. Bradley turned him over with his foot. "Yeah," he nodded, noting the broken face under the warpaint. "It's you. You happy now?" He gazed down at the twisted grimace and squirming body. "You were hell-bent on killin' an' destroyin'. Well, how does it feel, huh? This what you wanted, huh? You bastard!" The insane rage soared within him again. "This is what killin' is! You happy now? Aaaaagh!" He chopped fiercely with the bloodstained sabre and ended the life of the man who had hunted him so persistently.

He caught his horse and led him back to where the pack animals waited. Leaning in exhaustion against the flank of his hard-breathing mount blood welling from wounds in his neck and legs, he spoke to the uncomprehending animals.

"Didn' think I'd be here to do

this," he told them. "But it's jus' about over now . . . jus' about over. One more battle. One more score to settle . . . Then I guess we can call it a day."

10

HE studied the place carefully from safe cover but even with the field glasses he could not be sure. There was a sign nailed up on the wall of one of the shacks: it said 'Beek's Place' — or something like that . . . couldn't quite make it out. Could that be it? Yeah. Could be, he supposed. There weren't likely to be too many places in the area of Fort Laramie with a name like that. Still, he couldn't be absolutely sure. He'd have to go in there to find out, and that meant careful preparation.

He made his way back to where he'd left his horses and began to consider. His wounds would give him good cover . . . but he wouldn't take firearms with him: they'd be watching him closely if he did that. He'd stash the rifle and pistols somewhere where he could get them when he needed them — the sabre too. He glanced towards the bow and arrows and the two lances that were strapped on to the side of the pack-saddle. He'd picked them up from the last field of battle . . . he didn't know why . . . maybe because they were the best of their kind, like the single Indian skewbald pony that he had brought along. Should he take any of those? Yeah, why not? You never knew what might come in handy.

He sat down with his back to a tree and thought for a while and when he rose up he had it all figured out. He checked the rifle and pistols: all loaded and primed. He wrapped the rifle and one pistol in a piece of buffalo hide and hid them under some bushes. He'd have liked to be nearer the shacks, so that he could have got them more quickly, but he couldn't risk that. He stuck the remaining pistol in his belt, mentally marked the place, then mounted and rode back the way he had come, away from the shacks.

When he had gone about a mile he reined in, dismounted and unsaddled his pack-horse. Again, he hid the saddle bridle and other gear amongst bushes and turned the horse free to graze. He mounted his own horse, taking the bow, arrows and two lances with him, caught up the hackamore lead rope of the Indian pony and rode back towards Beek's Place, leading the pony behind him. He passed the place where he had hidden his guns, went a bit further then dismounted and hid the bow, arrows and lances. He heaved himself back into the saddle, his wounded leg throbbing bad, and, with the pony in tow, rode directly up to Beek's Place.

It was Bandy Greeley who spotted his approach. The little bow-legged man was leaning on the porch rail absently gazing out at the world. He reached for the Springfield rifle that leant against the wall behind him and shifted the quid of tobacco in his cheek. "Rider comin'," he called to the other occupants of the shack. "Got an Injun pony with him. Don't look much."

He raised the Springfield and pointed it roughly at the approaching rider. "Awright, that's far enough," he called. "Put ya hands in the air, an' keep 'em there till we get a look at ya. Kowalski!" he called. "Get out there an' take a look at this fella."

The tall, blond youth sauntered out and up to Bradley. "That the only gun you got?" he asked, nodding towards the pistol stuck in Bradley's belt. "Lemme have it — you got to, if'n you want to come in." Bradley surrendered the weapon. "You come far?" The pale, cold eyes surveyed him without real interest.

"Yeah, too far. From a stranded wagon train. Tryin' to get to Fort Laramie, but ran into a fight with some Shoshones." He indicated the blood-stiff bandages on his leg and neck. "Sure as hell could do with some grub an' a rest — an' maybe a little whisky?"

Kowalski was leading his horse by

the bridle towards the shacks. "He's okay," he called to Greeley. "Been in a fight with some Shoshones."

"Well, you can't be too careful out here," drawled the bow-legged little man as the pair reached the shack. He grinned sardonically at Bradley. "Fella that useta own this place taught us that."

"Yeah . . . but it didn' do him much good!" Kowalski put in. He looked at Greeley and a conspiratorial grin went between them.

"Come inside." Kowalski gestured with the pistol. It was as much a command as an invitation. Bradley dismounted stiffly and clumped up the steps and into the shack followed by the two men.

He had the impression of a big, ramshackle, dirty building with a bad smell, or a lot of bad smells. Half-eaten food littered the table; clothes, skins, boots and tools littered the floor. There was a heavy clumping and a fat, solid man entered from an adjoining room, buttoning up his pants. "What we got here?" His red-rimmed eyes studied Bradley challengingly.

"Fella been in a fight, with some Shoshones," explained Kowalski. "Needs a rest . . . got wounded, wants grub, whisky."

"Yeah?" The big man continued buttoning, not looking at Bradley. "But has he got any fuggin' money? This ain't the sailors' home." He turned to Greeley. "He got a gun?"

"Here, Pike." Kowalski held out the pistol.

"How'd you get into the Injun fight?" Burden turned back to Bradley. He weighed the pistol thoughtfully in one hand.

"Jus' ran into them. Jus' ridin' along and ran right into them, 'bout six of 'em." He didn't want his story to sound improbable.

"But you got away all right?" Burden was openly suspicious. "How'd that happen?"

"Didn' get away all right," said

Bradley. "Lost my rifle, an' my pack-horse. Goddam near got killed too." He nodded towards his leg wounds.

"But you got an Indian pony. Ain't that funny? Injuns don' usually give ponies away. How's that, heh?"

"Found him," answered Bradley. "Yesterday. Found him wanderin'. Don't know where he came from, but figgered I could trade him for some grub, ammunition . . . an' I sure do need a rest."

"Injun pony ain't no good to us," Burden shook his head dismissively. "We'll take your horse, an' saddle. You can keep the razorback. He'll carry you to Laramie. You eat what we eat, an' you'll get a little whisky — maybe a little piece of ass. What else you got to trade?"

"I ain't got nothin'. Like I said, I lost my pack-horse an' all my stuff. An' I can't trade my saddle horse . . . need it, bad . . . an' my saddle. Can let you have the pony . . . "

"I jus' tol' you the pony ain't no

fuggin' good." Burden stared at him, his voice low and threatening. "You wanna eat, an' rest, you give us the horse an' saddle . . . an' the pistol," he added, watching Bradley closely.

"But I need a gun!" protested Bradley. "I mean, I could run into trouble again . . . "

"Who says you ain't in trouble now?" Burden stood in front of him and tapped him on the chest with the pistol. Suddenly he seemed to change his mind. "We'll take your horse, an' saddle, an' your pistol." He spoke conclusively. "That'll be a fair trade. You can keep the razorback. You can eat with us, now. Fatstuff!" He yelled aloud. "Git some goddam grub on the table, if ya know what's good for ya!" He turned to Greeley. "Git that fuggin' red sow in here!"

There was no need for Greeley to do anything: a dirty, fat squaw hurried in from the adjoining shack. She wore an old duster coat down to her bare heels and nothing under it. Her face was disfigured by bruises, one eye swollen shut. She was plainly very frightened.

"Grub!" barked Burden. "An' fetch a little whisky. We got compn'y."

Fifteen minutes later they were all seated at the rickety table eating some kind of tough, sour meat together with pinto beans and cornpone. A jug of fierce, raw whisky went round and Bradley was plied with questions.

"How come you're way out this way?"

"Like I said, I was part of a wagon train, but we got stuck . . . people got sick. We hadda stay put a while, me an' Harry — Harry Embers, my partner."

"Harry who? Embers? Didja say Embers?" Burden looked up from his gnawing of a bone. "That the name?"

"Jesus! Don't tell me it was ol' Harry?" A grin of delight split Greeley's face. "Thin fella? Right arm cut up bad, with a knife? Scar on his fuggin' head? That the fella?"

"Yeah . . . " Bradley feigned confusion. "Yeah Harry was thin . . . an' he had a coupla scars . . . "

"Where the fug is he now then?" Burden was only mildly interested. He continued gnawing the bone like a dog.

"Harry? He's dead. Died of the fever. Why, you know him?"

Greeley grinned a malicious grin. "Let's say we useta know him. Was kinda . . . partners. But ol' Harry kinda lost his balls. After a little . . . house party." He laughed openly and Kowalski joined in. "Tol' us he was gonna get himself a wagon an' go to Cal'forny. I think maybe he got religion or som'pin. Wanted a wife an' family. 'What the hell!' I tol' him. 'They's plenty wives an' families aroun' . . . without you goin' back east for one.' But he wouldn' have it. Hadda go back east, get a wagon, turn honest. Jesus!" He shook his head in amused incomprehensibility. "What gets inta these fellas? Was the kid that did it, I guess."

"Kid? What kid? I don't understan'."

Bradley feigned confusion.

"Jus' a little bastard got in the way," grunted Greeley dismissively. "It don't matter. Ain't nothin' to do with you . . . you eat your dinner an' don' ask goddam questions."

"Where didja meet him — ol' Harry, I mean?" Burden threw the gnawed bone on to the floor and reached across to spear another hunk of meat from the tin dish in the centre of the table.

In Saint Jo . . . " Bradley stopped. It was his knife. Burden was using his knife — his, Joe Bradley's. He recognised it immediately, the knife Mary had bought him for their second anniversary. He could even see his own name engraved on the blade as Burden sawed and cut the rancid meat: 'Joe B.': it was all the engraver had had room for.

"In Saint Joseph, Missouri," he forced himself to say, then he half-folded up, in pain and grief and confusion. He didn't know how it happened: a great wave of weakness suddenly swept over him and he could do nothing about it.

"You sick?" Greeley looked at him suspiciously. "You ain't got the fuggin' fever? 'Cause if you have, Mister, you're on your fuggin' own . . . "

"Fever?" Burden looked up quickly. "You said Harry died of the fever. You got it? You bringin' it here?" He turned to Kowalski. "Get the bastard outside."

"Naw, I ain't got fever . . . it's these wounds. Didn' I tell you I jus' been in a fight with the Shoshones . . . I lost a lotta blood . . . I be okay . . . " Bradley fought against exhaustion.

"Get the bastard outside, Kowalski," repeated Burden anxiously. "Hey! Fat Bastard! Fatstuff!" He shouted for the squaw. "Get this fuggin' fella outside!"

"Where'll we put him, Pike?" Kowalski pushed himself away from the table and stood over Bradley.

"I don' fuggin' care where you put him, so as you get the bastard outa here. Put him in the goddam stable.

Throw him in the fuggin' creek, for all I care."

Bradley found himself being hauled up from the table. Then he was being half-carried, half-dragged across the dusty yard, Kowalski on one side, the fat, reeking squaw on the other. He was dumped in some damp straw in a tumbledown stable. Wind whistled through great holes in the woodwork; the pungent smell of horseshit was overwhelming. Somehow all his strength had deserted him — a reaction to the great demands he had made upon himself in recent weeks, perhaps, and the shock of seeing the knife, the final confirmation. Whatever it was, he could do nothing about it. He could only lie there. In a little while he had passed out completely.

He awoke in the middle of the night, lying where he had been dumped, but rested, his head clear. He rose slowly to his feet, testing his legs. He seemed to have recovered. He breathed deeply despite the thick air. Was he fit for what he had to do? He flexed his muscles, yes. He was. Had to be. Because he knew what he had to do, and there would never be a better opportunity to do it.

He stole cautiously out of the stable. The air was cool and damp. It had been raining. He made his way as quietly as he could, out of the yard, away from the shacks.

Safely away from the place he hurried to where he had left his guns and found them without difficulty. But as soon as he reached them he knew he was sunk: some animal had been worrying the buffalo hide covering he had wrapped them in; the guns were exposed to the weather — and the priming, and probably the charge — were damp, even wet. Useless to even try to fire them.

He straightened up. That wouldn't stop him. Nothing would stop him doing what he had to do. He hurried to where he had hidden the Indian weapons; dampness wouldn't affect them. He'd just have to change his plans, that was all.

He collected the bow, arrows and the two lances and stole silently back to the jumble of shacks. Everything still quiet. Everybody sleeping. Good job they had no dog. Dog would have given the alarm. Funny they didn't have a dog, out here . . .

No, goddammit! They weren't all sleeping! Someone was coming out of the main shack . . . a tall figure, stretching sleepily. Looked like Kowalski. What in hell was he doing up at this time?

As he stood silently watching, Kowalski began to trudge round the back of the main shack towards a privy some thirty yards away. Bradley breathed a sigh of relief. Yeah, that figgered. It gave him an even better opportunity, too.

He took off his boots and laid them on the ground along with the Indian weapons. Then, taking only one Indian lance with him, he hurried as quietly as he could into the yard. There was a hatchet there, beside the woodpile. He didn't want any noise from Kowalski; didn't want the others wakened — yet.

He reached the woodpile, found the hatchet. He hurried silently towards the privy. There, he paused. This was the moment. What was he going to do? Inside the privy he could hear the grunting and sighing of one of the men who had ravished his wife, killed his wife and son. What should he . . .

Before he could decide he heard Kowalski move and knew that he was coming out. Bradley stepped to the side of the privy and waited. The door creaked open. Kowalski, head bent, slouched out, barefoot, still hauling up his drawers. Bradley suddenly had a vision of his dead wife, his dead son, saw their tortured features. He stepped swiftly forward and swung the hatchet with all his strength, blunt edge forward. It caught Kowalski on the base of the skull with a sound like a sledgehammer hitting soft stone. Kowalski went down and stayed down. He squirmed slightly, like a crushed insect in its final death throes.

There was a sound from the shack. Someone was moving about. Greeley's voice came through the night: "Kowalski? That you? Where are ya? Ya okay?" There was further muttering. One voice or two? Bradley couldn't tell. Clouds were moving across the weak moon, now obscuring the light, now permitting some shifting illumination. He picked up the Indian lance and stepped into the shadow of an adjoining shack. He waited, motionless and silent.

There were soft, suspicious footsteps . . . a man in stockinged feet. "Kowalski? You there? Don' fug about now. Might be trouble." Greeley appeared on the porch. He wore only drawers and an undershirt and carried a Springfield rifle. He paused, half-turned as though to go back inside, then turned again and started to make his way towards the privy, the rifle held at the ready.

The soft snoring noise of the prostrate Kowalski reached his ears. He began to run towards it. The moon appeared from behind a cloud, lighting up the area with a sudden brilliance.

Bradley ran half a dozen steps and hurled the lance with all his might. Through the air it whistled for a brief second then the warhead speared Greeley through the kidneys, ploughing through the soft parts of his body and thrusting through his belly like a gory snout, the decorative feathers bristling bright blood. Greeley shouted like some unearthly ghost or spirit and the rifle went off in his hands as he sank on to the bloody earth, a few feet from the dying Kowalski.

Bradley ran now, openly and regardless of noise, to where he had left the other weapons. The big man would come out now, with a gun, or guns. He picked up the other lance, the bow and the arrows. Which was his best bet?

He had to wait a long time for Burden to appear. When the fat man did come out it was with great caution. He called many times from the shack, trying to get answers from Greeley or Kowalski. "Bandy? That you shootin'? What you shootin' at? You there Kowalski? What the fug's goin' on? You best come in. I ain't riskin' nothin'."

After a long time he appeared in the doorway, a rifle in his hands. For a long time he stood there, dressed, like Greeley, only in undershirt and drawers, reluctant to move any further. Bradley quietly laid down the lance, kept the bow and the arrows and moved silently into a position where he would be at Burden's back when the fat man did come out.

Burden was highly suspicious. He moved forward only a few wary inches, paused, looking all around. A few inches more . . . a couple of feet He was scenting trouble, stalking trouble . . . Now he was six feet from the door, his back exposed.

Bradley stepped silently round the

corner of the shack, an arrow notched to the bowstring. He drew the bow back as far as he could. His injured shoulder and neck throbbed and shuddered with the pain and effort. For a couple of seconds he held his aim steady then let fly. He heard the 'whorr' of the string then a distinct 'Thunk!' as the arrow thudded into the heavy body. There was a shocked gasp and the rifle dropped from Burden's hands. He twisted round just as Bradley loosed the second arrow. Again the 'whorr' and 'Thunk!' as the second shaft took him in the belly. He dropped the rifle and fell to his knees, then tumbled forward on to his front, the earth driving the second arrow deep into him.

The clouds drifted away, allowing the moon to illuminate the scene. Bradley walked to where Burden lay.

"It was you . . . you . . . I mighta fuggin' knowed." Burden spoke in anguished, gasping sighs. He was genuinely puzzled. "What the fug . . . What didja do that for . . . We wasn't gonna kill ya . . . jus' the fuggin' horse we was gonna take . . . like I tol' ya . . . Aw, Jesus! Do som'pin willya! I'm in fuggin' agony! Git these fuggin' arrows outa . . . "

"I killed you on account of my wife, an' son," Bradley explained. His voice was remote, matter-of-fact. "Your little 'house party' back in Kansas, at Saint Aubrey. Remember?"

Burden stared at him with uncomprehending eyes.

"Kowalski's dead. I killed him. And Greeley. I killed all of them. On account of my wife and son."

"For Jesus' sake kill *me*, willya! Ain't . . . no way for a white man . . . to die . . . these hellish fuggin' arrows . . . " Burden's hands, wet and red, were clasped round the broken arrow shafts that stuck out of his belly.

Bradley stood there, barefoot in the moonlight, the enormity of what he had done sinking slowly into his consciousness. Burden's agonized gasps sounded in his ears; further off he could hear the desperate moanings of Greeley, the snorings of Kowalski. Slowly he bent down, picked up the fallen rifle and shot Burden through the head.

* * *

The five wagons were just where he had left them, but there was a different atmosphere about them. Things had been tidied up and the stock in the little corral looked fit and healthy. The girl, Mary Maxwell, saw him coming and came to meet him. "You came back," she greeted him. "You're just in time. We're thinking of going on to California."

"I wouldn't try that, not right now. Better to winter at Fort Laramie, then join a big wagon train from there in the spring."

"You sound like you've figured it all out." She smiled warmly at him.

"I have. I thought I'd take the wagon Mister Embers left me . . . "

"It's ready." Again the warm smile.

"I cleaned it up, sterilized everything. I wasn't sure whether you'd come back for it . . . I thought you had a place somewhere already . . . "

"I had . . . or I thought I had. But I wouldn't stay here, in this . . . wilderness. I've had enough of it. The cost of stayin' alive is too high out here, much too high. I want to live amongst civilized people."

They had reached the wagon that was now his. It was clean and orderly inside and smelled like a hospital ward.

"Your Paw all right now? And the others?"

"Yes. They're all recovered. Ready to go. I think they'll take your advice — about wintering at Fort Laramie, I mean. And I think they'd like to have you come along."

"What do *you* think? You think it's a good idea?" He was standing very close to her, could feel the clean warmth of her. He remembered that she was a woman of quality.

She nodded and came a fraction

closer. "Yes. I think it's a good idea. We can make a new start there."

"Uh-huh." He hesitated, pushing out of his mind the memories of the horrific things he had done — had had to do. "Well, I guess that, as long as a man is alive, it's never too late to make a new start. But in Californy: not here. Not in this savage land."

She nodded sympathetically. "I agree. Not here. In California. Where there's some civilization."

"Civilization." He nodded. "That's for me. I've had enough of barbarism, lot more than a bellyful."

He reached gently out and took her arm and together they began to walk to her father's wagon — and the beginnings of a new start.